With Love in Their Corner

The Boxers of Brook Street
Book 1

Sandra Sookoo

ARE YOU SIGNED UP FOR DRAGONBLADE'S BLOG?

You'll get the latest news and information on exclusive giveaways, exclusive excerpts, coming releases, sales, free books, cover reveals and more.

Check out our complete list of authors, too!

No spam, no junk. That's a promise!

Sign Up Here

www.dragonbladepublishing.com

Dearest Reader;

Thank you for your support of a small press. At Dragonblade Publishing, we strive to bring you the highest quality Historical Romance from some of the best authors in the business. Without your support, there is no 'us', so we sincerely hope you adore these stories and find some new favorite authors along the way.

Happy Reading!

CEO, Dragonblade Publishing

Additional Dragonblade books by Author Sandra Sookoo

The Boxers of Brook Street Series
With Love in Their Corner (Book 1)

The Hasting Sisters Series
The Devil's Game (Book 1)
A Second Summertime Courtship (Book 2)
An Impossible Match (Book 3)

Willful Winterbournes Series
Romancing Miss Quill (Book 1)
Pursuing Mr. Mattingly (Book 2)
Courting Lady Yeardly (Book 3)
Guarding the Widow Pellingham (Book 4)
Bedeviling Major Kenton (Book 5)
Charming Miss Standish (Book 6)
Teasing Miss Atherby (Novella)

The Storme Brother Series
The Soul of a Storme (Book 1)
The Heart of a Storme (Book 2)
The Look of a Storme (Book 3)
The Sting of a Storme (Book 4)
The Touch of a Storme (Book 5)
The Fury of a Storme (Book 6)
Much Ado About a Storme (Novella)
A Storme's First Noelle (Novella)
A Storme's Christmas Legacy (Novella)

The Lyon's Den Series
The Lyon's Puzzle
The Lyon's Redemption
Dreaming of a Lyon

Chapter One

March 13, 1817
Stapleton House
Marylebone, Mayfair
London, England

L EWIS STAPLETON, EIGHTH Earl of Lethbridge, stood by one of the windows in his drawing room with a cut crystal glass of brandy in his hand and a frown tugging at the corners of his mouth. The shadows of twilight were just descending, and in an hour, he, his mother, and his brothers would scatter for the evening's entertainments.

Yet it seemed they hadn't had enough of bedeviling him for the evening. And if he hadn't loved her dearly, he would have quit the townhouse by now.

"Lewis, listen to me. Instead of spending all your time at the club, you should accept the wealth of invitations sitting on your desk and start mingling in society," his mother said with a slight frown. She took a sip from the teacup. "You have just turned three and thirty, but you have no marriage plans on the horizon. That is unacceptable."

"According to who, Mama?" He took a deep sip of the brandy. "You or the society gossips you keep company with?"

"Don't take that snippy tone with me, young man." She patted her upswept light brown hair that contained a few silver strands while his younger brothers exchanged amused glances. "I have known you all your life and you have always been stubborn. Ever since your father died, it's grown worse."

"That is not my fault." His jaw worked as he contemplated his next words. "Papa didn't have a head for business, and he was an even worse gambler." What was more, none of the family had known just what a mess of the books he'd made until after his sudden death two years ago this month.

Damn, had it been two years already?

"Don't blame your father for the current circumstances." The sharpness in his mother's voice stood as testament to the fact the family as a whole hadn't quite put anger and grief behind them like they wanted others to think. "It wasn't his fault."

Lewis snorted. "Pray, tell me whose fault it was then." He knocked back the remainder of the brandy and swallowed it in one go. The burn of the liquor in his throat only distracted him slightly. "None of us were allowed to set foot in his study or even look at the account books. His man-of-affairs was forbidden to consult with us—with me as the heir—on any financial matter."

"Your father didn't wish to burden you boys with problems that came up."

"No, he didn't want to let on that things were spinning out of control for him, and he wanted to cover it for as long as he could." In some annoyance, he set his empty glass on a nearby round table. "It doesn't matter now. I've been handed a title I only grudgingly wanted this early in my life and nearly empty coffers. None of that makes me want to rush out and pledge my suit to a woman. It's not fair to ask someone to share this life until I can puzzle out a way to restore the family fortune."

"But you have a responsibility to that title, Lewis," his mother said with a raised eyebrow. "You need a son to carry on the succession. You have always known that."

Of course he had. From the age of ten, it had been drilled into him that he would be the earl at some point. He just never thought it would be this early or that his father would have been taken suddenly from this world by a blow to the head in an illegal bare-knuckle boxing match.

"I am well aware, but with a pile of debt, a crumbling manor in the country, and nearly empty coffers? Who would want to marry me with a basically empty title?" It was an argument they indulged in every two or three months and had since his father was brought back to London, bloodied and barely breathing. By the time they'd had a physician in, his father had passed from injuries sustained to his head from multiple blows.

It couldn't be categorized as murder since he left the ring under his own power, and boxing for sport or payment was highly illegal, thus the reason such matches could never be held in London proper. Despite his father being a prize fighter and all his bouts highly anticipated, none of them could be advertised, which meant supporters of the sport stayed apprised of such things through taverns, brothels, and clubs. This tended to make the crowds swell. To say nothing of the fact that his opponent had been a duke, and therefore untouchable by law.

Or anything else.

His mother blew out a breath of frustration. Clearly, she didn't want to hear his excuses any longer. "Marry a young heiress. She'll not care about anything except the title, then you'll have the coin and a fertile wife who will give you many children."

Bloody hell.

Briefly, he pointed his gaze to the ceiling, and when the sound of rain against the windowpane reached his ears, he transferred his regard outside once more. "What makes you think I want to perpetuate this line?"

"It is tradition," his mother said with shock in her tone.

"What if it's not mine?" Then he turned about and encompassed his brothers into his gaze. The middle one was two years younger than him, and the youngest was two years behind him. They all looked as if they could have been triplets if one wasn't peering too closely. "Perhaps one of you two can take up those reins."

Even if that wasn't possible unless something dire happened to him.

Alexander, his middle brother, scoffed. As he folded a copy of *The Times*, he addressed Lewis' statement. "I want nothing to do with the title, and I'm just the spare regardless." He glanced at their mother. "No offense, Mama, but you and I both know that Papa doted on Lewis, couldn't wait to train him in how to run things. That truly tainted such responsibility for me."

Over the years, there had been underlying rivalry between Lewis and his brothers. They'd all understood where they'd ranked in the pecking order and why, and since there were no sisters to temper the urge to work out frustrations in rough and tumble ways, they'd grown into adulthood with varying degrees of resentment, anger, jealousy, and envy that had never been addressed before their father had died.

The one thing their father had been adamant he pass down to all three boys was his skill in boxing. One weekend a month, he would take them out into Hyde Park and simulate matches, and since their father was a prize fighter of some acclaim, those outings were rigorous, and somewhat humiliating. Yes, he trained his boys in the upstairs private parlor, but there was just something about being put out into the open and pitted against each other that a home version of boxing couldn't give.

Their mother frowned. She laid her teacup and its saucer on the low table in front of her. "How disappointing it is to know that my sons are willing to turn their backs on everything their father held dear." Mild aggravation threaded through her tone. "I thought you'd been raised better than that."

Ah, good, the guilt has made an appearance. I'd wondered when that would happen.

Lewis snorted. "If Papa had truly held his property, his fortune, and his family dear, he wouldn't have gambled so heavily." That was the bald truth.

"Don't disrespect his memory," his mother snapped with narrowed eyes.

"Why not? He certainly disrespected us. Committed family man my arse."

"Lewis Arthur!" With her lips set in a tight line, his mother stood while his brothers looked on in varying degrees of shock. "You should be ashamed of yourself. Do you even care that I, at least, am still grieving?"

Immediately contrite, he nodded. "I'm sorry. That was insensitive of me." With a tight chest, he crossed the room to buss her cheek. "My dispute with Papa and my brothers has nothing to do with you." Since he hadn't had the time or wherewithal to process his anger, grief, or even fear of the future, he relied on the boxing outlet to relieve the pressure. At least it put the skills his father had instilled to good use.

Not that his mother knew that.

"Thank you for realizing that." She frowned at him. "Please promise you'll think about what I said. No matter your feelings, you need a wife. Sooner rather than later, for if I learned anything from your father's untimely passing, it is that life is short. We are not promised tomorrow."

"Good point." After bouncing his gaze between his brothers, he huffed. He might not be as good as them at boxing, but he'd won more than his share of illegal bouts and those purses had been nothing to sneeze at. "Perhaps I should go full time into boxing. Start touring around England, perhaps Ireland. I could win a decent amount, then wouldn't need to marry—heiress or otherwise."

Alexander chuckled. "That is a singularly horrid idea. Your shoulder can't take many more hits, and your knee is nearly shot." While he enjoyed doing a bout or two, Lewis didn't believe his brother's heart was in it like their father's had been. But since Alex hadn't found his path in life, this was what he filled his time with.

"They aren't so bad," he said, but even he heard the doubt in his voice. Was it a trick of the mind, for his left shoulder held a dull throb. He could no longer ignore that it had been dislocated more than a few times.

His brother huffed and crossed his arms at his chest. "Don't be a nodcock, Lewis. If any of your opponents get wind of these weaknesses, your arse will be lying on that field, and the reputation of our name will be ruined."

"It won't be ruined," he maintained, with a bit of annoyance in his tone. As for his right knee, that might prove to be more of a problem than the shoulder, but as long as he didn't put weight on it during a match and made no sudden changes in trajectory, he would be fine.

Hopefully.

Finally, his youngest brother added his opinion. "That name is the only thing Papa left us." Duncan was suave and sophisticated, but a rakehell and a horrible manager of money. His pockets were always to let, which meant he was forever asking for coin from Lewis. He was great at boxing, almost to the point of cockiness, and had natural talent. Out of all of them, he took after their father in skill and point at a bout. "Don't take that away from us merely because you are unable to square with how you felt about him. Weren't your last words to him ones of anger?"

"Yes." Lewis bit off the urge to respond with a biting comment. He didn't wish to remember his final conversation with his father; he'd told no one the subject matter of that discussion, but he had admitted it wasn't anything kind.

"You only care about the prize purses boxing brings. You don't give two braces about the family name or the estates." No, that responsibility fell to his shoulders and his alone. Sometimes the weight was enormous. His chest tightened, and the need to work through that stalled emotion grew nearly overwhelming.

"Do you blame us?" Duncan flashed a grin. As he leaned back in his chair, he rested an ankle on a knee. The knot of his cravat had been loosened, but somehow, it only made him more attractive in his evening clothes. "Boxing is a lucrative endeavor if one has the skill and doesn't take themselves too seriously."

"Then you think to base the whole of your life on it? In the hopes you collect enough prize money to fund your life, such as it is?" His little brother had taken rooms at the Albany while he apparently sought to live his rakish lifestyle to the hilt.

"I'm damn well going to try."

Lewis shook his head. "A nodcock idea at best."

"As if your way of living is having better results?" One of Duncan's eyebrows rose in challenge. "If you don't get out from under all of this, brother, you are going to break."

His hold on his control slipped. "And how do you propose I do that, hmm? I'm the damned earl, the current holder of this title, the head of this family, and all I receive for my efforts is complaints and badgering." Unable to settle, Lewis shoved a hand through his hair. "I haven't been my own man since Papa died, perhaps before then, and I don't mind telling you that I feel trapped."

Would he give up everything his family stood for out of pique? Unlikely, but that didn't relieve the annoyance stuck firmly in his chest.

"Stop this talk. All of you." His mother clapped her hands until all three of them glanced at her. "I want you to leave the silly notion of boxing behind you." She met each of their gazes. "Go out and make honest livings and stop stirring the scandalbroth. I would like to attend a society function without hearing at least a snatch of gossip concerning you three." Then she rested her regard on Lewis. "I mean it, Lewis. Stop dithering and find a lady to court. I want you engaged by year's end."

He and his brothers all offered protests at once, and the clamor of voices quickly filled the room.

Lewis held up a hand for quiet. "While I understand your concern, Mama, I don't understand why I can't enjoy both responsibility and pleasure." As it was, it felt as if he would soon be torn between duty and happiness.

For long moments, she held his gaze, her expression unyielding. "Your father's death was difficult for me, as was finding out the truth regarding our finances and future. You are the oldest son, and I am counting on you to make things right. That is how it is, regardless of how you feel about it, or your father." She moved across the carpet to lay a hand briefly on his arm. "Don't disappoint me, Lewis. I don't know how much more I can withstand before breaking." Sadness shadowed her hazel eyes that were like his. "This is what titled men must do."

And more weight was subtly added to his shoulders.

But he didn't have the luxury of breaking, for a man like him had to remain strong and stoic. Hadn't his father always taught him that? He gave her a curt nod, and hated that his brothers looked on with curiosity and pity. "If I promise to attend more society functions and meet more eligible women in the hopes one of them might make an impression on me, will you stop nagging me to marry and set up a nursery?"

"Perhaps." She shrugged. "If I don't talk about it, you'll forget or completely ignore me, but I promise you the space to order your life as you see fit. At least until late autumn. After that we will need to talk seriously." Again, she glanced at the three of them. "Have a good night, boys, and remember what I said."

Then she exited the room.

With a huff, Lewis retrieved his glass. "Can I pour anyone a brandy?" Definitely, he could use another.

Alexander shook his head as he gained his feet. "I'll have one at the club. Suddenly, I don't feel like lingering here any longer."

"Fair enough." When Lewis gained the sideboard, he splashed a measure of the amber liquid into his glass and then replaced the decanter. "I don't want to enter into a courtship just now, fellows."

"Then don't," Duncan said with a negligent shrug.

"You heard her. I don't have much of a choice."

Alexander snorted. "Then find a way to bring in quick coin. If Mama sees the coffers filling, she'll go lighter on the need for you to marry an heiress."

"How, though? As you said, my fighting in bouts is finite at best." After a few sips of brandy, he suddenly perked up as a new thought occurred to him. "What about this? You can't deny we are all knowledgeable about boxing. So why don't we open a boxing salon?"

"What?" Alexander gawked.

"Bloody brilliant," Duncan exclaimed as he sprang from his chair.

Lewis nodded as he grinned. "It will be a way to make coin, and we'll offer our skills to everyone. I don't want there to be a class divide. Payments can be worked out, but as long as their accounts are current, the business will prove solvent."

"Interesting concept." Alexander cocked his head to one side. "However, why would anyone want to come to our salon when Gentleman Jackson has his own? And he's much more popular than the three of us put together."

"Speak for yourself," Duncan said with a confident smirk. "Our father was a prize fighter. That is our hook. He taught us everything he knew, and there are three of us with different skill sets. Additionally, Alex can do the books in the beginning. Everyone from all walks of life might find themselves needing to defend themselves or wish to learn how to box. Unless I miss my guess, it will soon be all the rage as a sport of entertainment."

"This is true. With every bout, the crowds grow." Excitement lit Duncan's face. "We can open the salon in Mayfair, somewhere on Brook Street to capitalize on the rich nobs in the area."

Alexander nodded. "Yes, and put it over a legitimate shop. Shoes, for example. We can own the building and have an income stream from that, but it won't be readily known there is a salon unless one is in the know." His grin was as wide as Duncan's. "We'll teach boxing, self-defense, physical fitness, balance, whatever the client might need. Boxing is only the draw, but there are many skills that go into that one discipline."

"Agreed," Lewis said with a nod. Perhaps his outlook wasn't as bleak as he'd assumed. "How does one find out if there is available shop space?"

"I'll take care of it." Alexander shot them both a look. "I have some connections, and there are always shops that have defaulted on their rents."

"Excellent." Duncan came over to Lewis, took his brandy glass, drained the contents, and then handed it back. "I will use my considerable charm as I go through society to bring clients to our establishment once it's open. Lewis can be the principal instructor until the rest of us have the time. We'll need a few tick mattresses for falls and tumbling, some padded mittens for beginners, and go from there."

Slowly, Lewis nodded. "Will we take female clients?"

Alexander frowned. "I can't imagine how that could happen without causing plenty of scandal."

"And Mama won't like that," Duncan added in the world's worst stage whisper.

"All true." He blew out a breath. "What of advertising?"

Duncan's grin was wicked. "We will talk the salon up. Make it sound exclusive. Stapleton Boxing Salon. Open weekdays. One evening we can remain open late for those who can't make the daytime hours. We can even take special lessons upon request for an additional fee."

"Good points." Lewis grinned. "It can't fail."

"Indeed," Alexander said, with a grin of his own. "And the lower impact of instruction should keep you more or less intact a bit longer." Yet he exchanged a glance of worry with Duncan. Clearly, the two were concerned. "But first, we'll need the property and the equipment: mattress ticks, sandbags, padded mittens, all the other things Papa had us use when he gave us our first lessons."

"Good." Lewis shoved his own worry deep down inside to ponder later. "At least this is forward movement. In six months we might be better off for it."

And perhaps having something else to focus on would give him time to think about what he wanted for his life, for one thing was certain: he refused to have his life end as his father's had. When he left this mortal coil, he wanted to leave his family better than they were now.

The hows of accomplishing that escaped him at the moment.

Chapter Two

May 23, 1817
Dawson's Imports
Robinhood Lane
East India Dock
London, England

MISS CECILIA DAWSON totaled up a column of numbers, wrote the sum at the bottom of the page, and then blew on the page until the ink dried. There was something so satisfying about balancing a ledger book and making certain nothing had taken a loss. But her father's importing business was quite healthy, and he was doing well.

The space was quite cozy for an office. Lead-paned glass windows occupied the bulk of one wall from the middle to the ceiling, which let in loads of natural light and overlooked the East India Dock. Some days she let her imagination run away with her as she watched the ships either come into their berths or leave for parts unknown. What it must be like to have the freedom to sail the seas and have adventures.

Aside from the massive desk she worked at, there were two leather wingback chairs facing that piece of furniture. A colorful rug in an Oriental style covered the hardwood floor. In one corner, a golden birdcage rested. Currently, there was no bird inside, but at one time her father had a parrot that had obtained a rather bad habit for swearing. A sideboard and shelves in dark stain to match the desk rested against the other walls of the office, all containing maps and other paperwork pertaining to her father's travels all over the world, as well as the locations he procured his wares from.

This office had become a haven of sorts, especially since her mother had died eleven years ago. Her father was the one constant in her life, and each time she came into the space, her soul settled. If she tried hard enough, she could still smell the tobacco he used to smoke when he had his pipe. The scents of leather, as well as a few exotic spices from a basket of dried potpourri he'd obtained from India also reached her nose, and she smiled, for when she was a child, her father always used to tell her about it. "In the twelfth century, potpourri was used to freshen castle rooms and mask the smells of medieval times. Spices and herbs were doused in spirits and left to rot, creating a pungent but pleasant aroma." Then he would grin and his eyes would sparkle as if he knew a fantastic secret he couldn't wait to share. "In fact, Ceci, the word potpourri comes from the French 'pot pourri' meaning rotten pot."

It was one of the reasons he was adamant she keep current on her language skills.

But then, he had always been a fascinating person. As for herself, she was content in doing the accounting for his office. At seven and twenty, she felt no driving need to make a name for herself or to set London on its ear because of something she'd done. Additionally, she wasn't one of those women who wasn't happy unless she was chasing scandal or finding new ways to entice men into shadowy corners merely for the sensation or shock.

Not that any of that was nonsense, but for her, it just wasn't necessary to live a fulfilling life. Of course, that was subject to change every day depending on her mood, but for now, she was content.

When the door to the office opened, she glanced up to greet

the newcomer, but then relaxed when she saw it was her eleven-year-old brother, born when she was sixteen. Their mother had perished while struggling to give birth to the later-in-life boy, and she felt a special sort of bond with him since he'd never known a mother's love.

"I thought you were with your tutor? Isn't this afternoon for languages?" she asked, as the tan and black pug pulled at his leather lead ahead of her brother.

The blond-haired boy scoffed and frowned. "You know how I detest learning languages. Besides, Mr. Kinnett has no sense of humor; his lessons are rather dry. I'd much rather walk Archimedes."

"I don't blame you. He's a well-mannered dog, and I'll let you in on a secret. I struggled with Latin as well as French. Still do, but then, folks don't usually go about conversing in Latin." She shrugged. "It's useful for reading old documents and maps, though."

"Then why do you bother me with the learning of such?"

"Why? Because it is a skill like anything else, and if you truly wish to become a sailor, it will serve you will eventually." It was a worry she'd always carried around, ever since the boy had announced that intention when he'd been a lad of seven and he finally figured out what their father did for a living and why he'd been gone so much.

"Bah. It's annoying." He dropped the lead, and the pug decided to wander about the shipping office, sniffing into corners and behind furniture. "There is so much I could be doing instead. Exploring, even."

"Such as getting into trouble or running amok over the docks?" Though she loved her little brother dearly, he didn't need to mix with some of the men who worked in the area. They were a rough and tumble set, and more often than not they had mischief and mayhem on their minds.

To say nothing of the fact that she felt more and more unsafe when she needed to find a hired hack whenever she wished to go home to Mayfair. Thank the heavens they no longer lived in the few rooms above the shipping office. It was bad enough merely being here, and sometimes alone, for some of the bolder men thought nothing of harassing her. As she'd grown older, she didn't trust them, especially since those men were only interested in getting under her skirts.

A flush colored James' cheeks. "Some of them are interesting."

"That very well may be so, but most are merely trouble. I don't want you falling in with them and ruining your future." She closed the ledger book, then stowed it into one of the drawers in the stout wooden desk she sat behind. "This life is difficult enough without you deliberately seeking out problems, and I don't have the wherewithal at times to pull you out of them."

In many ways, though she felt responsible for her little brother as a mother might, she yearned to have her own life, one that had nothing to do with the shipping outfit or caring for a child that wasn't hers.

"I don't want the trouble." The boy frowned as he dropped into a leather chair that faced the desk. In her mind's eye, she pictured her father sitting behind the massive desk, and when she'd been a young girl a couple of years older than James, she used to visit the office in what she called an adventure, for being at the docks was much different than anything she'd known in Mayfair. "I just want to do something exciting, and Papa says I'm too young to learn how to sail."

"I did say that, and I stick to it," their father said as he came into the office from a back room that was used to store overflow cargo that hadn't yet been sold or claimed. "When you are thirteen, then we shall talk. Until then, concentrate on your schooling. You won't get far in this life dumb as a broken slate with dull chalk."

Cecilia smiled. "Where are you off to, Papa? You look quite handsome."

Her father was a large presence in her life. Possessed of a

barrel chest, stout limbs, and a head of thick, blond hair, he was rather like the image of pirates portrayed in storybooks, except his light hair and ready grin belied that likeness. With eyes the color of a cornflower, he was still popular with the ladies whenever he consented to mingle within society.

"I have a meeting with a potential new client. If all goes well, it could prove lucrative for my business, which means I'll have more coin to invest into a dowry for you," he said as he leveled his gaze on her.

A groan escaped her. "Not this again." She ignored the snicker that came from James.

"Yes, this again." Her father bent and scooped up the pug, who thanked him by licking his cheek with exuberance. "You are seven and twenty, my girl. A spinster in some circles. I wish you would find a man and settle down so I won't need to worry over you."

She blew out a breath of frustration. "Do stop. I am not going to marry just for the sake of being married and then find out later the man is a bounder. Or have you forgotten what happened with my engagement?"

"Of course I haven't, but you can't push other men away out of fear of one."

"True."

A shiver moved down her spine. When she had been nineteen, she'd gotten engaged to a young man whom her father had sworn was a decent chap. Turned out, he truly wasn't. In fact, the man had a bit of a temper when things didn't go his way, and he took out his frustrations on her. More than once, she'd have bruises that she was forced to hide beneath her clothing, or if they were on her face, she'd invent wild stories as to why.

Eventually, her father figured out what was happening. He threatened the man within an inch of his life and had run him off. She had no idea where he was now, but she suspected he hadn't gone far from London; he simply had no ambition.

"However, you need to marry, Cici. I don't want you to look

back upon your life and have regrets because you delayed." With a wry smile, he scratched the dog behind its ears. "If I had my druthers, I would like to see you married to a rich nob who would keep you in high style. You deserve to be pampered. Haven't I always told you *ton* society would adore you? From everything I've seen this year, your looks are in."

Was that supposed to make her agree to do the gauntlet of society's balls and routs again? She'd had a Season when she was nineteen that had netted her a nightmare. Under no circumstances did she want that again for her life.

Not wanting to argue with him on that point, she nodded. "I understand that, but I'd rather be alone than beaten, talked down to, spend the next twenty years of my life pregnant, or treated with no respect." There weren't many options available to women in their world, whether one had coin, titles, or not.

"Be that as it may, there are good men out there. I'm going to increase your dowry to attract a wider pool of men. Some aristocrats need coin to stave out empty coffers. And you will be elevated in society to give you opportunities I can't bring you."

"Ha!" She shook her head as she glanced at James, who rolled his eyes. "And have a pity marriage, a union without love? No thank you."

Not that she was an expert in love. When she was engaged, she'd been young and naïve, but he was persuasive, charming, and frightened her a bit with his possession. Eventually, he'd convinced her to let him bed her. Which she did in one of the rooms upstairs in this very office, but the coupling was over before she could acclimate to it or find pleasure therein. Thankfully, a pregnancy didn't result in the joining, for her menses came the next day, and the rest of their relationship had been fraught with problems. Never had she told her father of that, for he would have killed her fiancé for certain.

Since that time, she'd tucked away her hurt and loneliness and come to work for her father. It wasn't a good life all the time, but it was life nonetheless. Looking after her father was a labor of love. He'd never been the same after losing her mother. And James needed her as well. How could she leave the two of them to their own devices merely to take a chance on marriage?

Standing up from the desk, she laid a hand on his arm. "I shall be fine. Don't worry about me so much. I will marry when the time is right and if I meet the right man." She flashed him a grin. "If you do worry, place that upon James. He'll prove more of an issue than I ever would."

"Unfair!" Her brother sprang up from his chair. "I'm just looking for a good time."

Their father chuckled, and the rich sound was as comforting now as it had been in her childhood. "Though truer words have never been spoken, they also can usher in a man's—or boy's—bad luck." He shoved Archimedes into her arms. "Come with me to my meeting. It might be a more useful way to enhance your education. If all goes well, we can start incorporating such things into your curriculum."

"Truly?" Excitement lit the boy's blue eyes.

"Of course. I am many things, but a liar I am not." He winked at Cecilia. "Are you finished here? I've the carriage waiting out front."

"I have a few invoices to finish here, then I have an errand to a bookshop. There is a book I'm hoping to grab secondhand in Mayfair before going home."

"Fair enough. You were always one to improve your mind with reading." He glanced at his son. "You could learn much from your sister." Then he looked at her again. "Stay vigilant and I will see you for dinner." Then he left the office with James in tow.

An hour later, Cecilia finished her work. With the leather lead wound about one hand and her reticule hung at her wrist, she drew the drapes closed on the downstairs windows, closed and then locked the door, and started off, walking past other shipping outfits and various warehouses that sat along the East India Dock. Archimedes found the adventure stimulating, for he stopped every few feet to sniff at a wooden pylon or corner of a building. Once, he paused to piddle on a coil of rope.

Not that she blamed him for wishing to explore or cavort. It was a beautiful May afternoon where the sun peeked out from clouds to shimmer on the water. With a slight chill in the spring air but with the scent of growing things in the background, it was one of those days when a person felt alive and had hope in their heart that anything could happen.

Just as she neared the end of the street that led away from the docks, a man exited one of the warehouses. When he saw her, he immediately came toward her, and since he was a hulking sort of person, Archimedes began barking at the intruder.

Ordinarily, she would caution the dog to quiet, but today, as foreboding prickled over her skin, she let him have at it. No matter that she continued on her walk, the man followed. Eventually, he dropped one heavy hand on her shoulder, which essentially halted her forward movement.

"Putting on so many airs that you're too good enough to talk with the likes of me?"

Briefly, she closed her eyes and prayed for patience and courage. Then she physically removed his hand from her person and turned to face him. "Ah, Mr. Derrickson. Don't you have something to occupy your time? Surely you don't need to accost me." Though her words were this side of bold, her stomach quivered with fear. But something must be done. He tried to delay her at least once a week.

"I don't need to but I'm going to until you talk to me." As he spoke, he advanced on her, causing Cecilia to retreat. "You are the sort of woman I want to take to wife."

Perish the thought.

"Then you should look elsewhere. I don't wish to marry anyone just now." When her back connected to the wall of a building, she inwardly groaned in dismay. There was nowhere to run, and she doubted if push came to shove that her pug would put up much of a fight.

"Don't want someone else. I want you." Mr. Derrickson planted a palm to the boards at the side of her head and leaned into her, so close that she could discern the scar on the left side of his face and smell the garlic and onions on his breath. "If you don't agree, I can't say what might happen to that beanpole of your brother."

She gasped as Archimedes hid behind her skirting. "Are you threatening James?"

"Clever, aren't you?" He leaned into her. "Now, give me a kiss so I can show you why you should marry me." Before she could react, he pressed his lips to hers, and the hold on her control snapped.

With a hard shove to his chest, she ducked away from him as soon as there was space between them. "Are you mad? I said I wasn't interested."

"You should be. Ain't getting any younger. Doing you a favor by offering." When he tried to embrace her, she shoved a knee into the soft flesh between his legs. Immediately, he doubled over with a groan.

Her heartbeat raced so quickly she feared her heart would jump out of her chest. "When I said no, I truly meant it, you ogre." Then, picking up her dog and tucking him beneath her arm, Cecilia fled along the street, never stopping until she reached the place where carriages for hire waited at the entrance to the docks.

Still shaking from her reaction, she engaged one of the drivers, and once she was safely inside the cab, she held the pug on her lap and frowned. She couldn't keep living like this. There were far too many horrid men in the world who required comeuppance or at the very least some incentive to leave her alone.

By the time she was dropped in Mayfair at the bookshop, she had managed to will herself into some semblance of calm, but not even wandering the stacks of Mr. Tetlow's bookshop could take the foul taste of that unwanted kiss from her mouth.

When she exited the shop with a book in hand, her gaze happened to land on a shop that sat kitty-corner from the bookseller. According to a sign in the front window, the shoemaker shop planned to open next month, but that wasn't what had arrested her notice. In much smaller letters on a second-floor window, a painter on a ladder was putting the finishing touches on lettering that read Stapleton Boxing Salon.

How interesting. Could that be the answer to her problems?

A chill twisted down her spine, and as she watched, a man around her age paused on the pavement in front of the shoe shop. His light brown hair curled at his collar but he chatted easily with the painter and the man who held the ladder. Was he the owner of the shoe shop or the boxing salon? It was difficult to tell, and she didn't have the courage to cross the street in order to ask.

But one thing was certain: this might just be what she'd been hoping and praying for. Picking up her dog, she whispered to him, "I'm going to visit that boxing salon, Archimedes, and I don't care if they won't grant me access. I'll dress as a boy if I must, but one way or another, I will learn how to defend myself."

Because Archimedes was naught but a dog, he uttered a low yap and then licked her cheek. Taking that as agreement and encouragement, Cecilia walked in the opposite direction from the shop in the direction of home.

I refuse to be a victim again.

Chapter Three

June 18, 1817
Stapleton Boxing Salon
Mayfair, London

Lewis glanced through the long space that was the Stapleton Boxing Salon. Occupying the upper floor above a shoe seller's shop, he and his brothers had worked for the last three months making the salon everything that they could ever want with their father's teachings in mind.

The hardwood floor gleamed, and the windows that looked out over Brook Street let in copious amounts of natural light. Along the far wall, punching bags hung from the ceiling. Two contained hard-packed straw while the other two contained sand for more advanced boxers. Occupying the middle portion of the floor were four mattress ticks or pallets where instruction would occur, and they would provide padding if a client continued to fall or was sent to the floor. That was part of the learning process. Toward the door were two wooden structures to resemble a man's form, wrapped with linen and padded so a student could practice their hooks and jabs. If the facial features drawn somewhat crudely on one of the oval-shaped faces loosely resembled himself, Lewis didn't care. His brothers sometimes had a warped sense of humor.

Whatever helped a client hone their skills.

And at the back of the room, in front of the office's windows, was a roped off section of floor where practice bouts would be held. It would prove a good way for clients to have a feel for a match and show them exactly how many feet of space they'd have to work with.

At the rear of the space was an office where he interviewed potential clients who wanted private boxing lessons. Unlike Gentleman Jackson's Salon, they weren't providing instructional classes for men who wandered in off the street. Their business model was based on appointment-only private lessons three times a week. On one of those evenings, they offered what they called "bout class" and that simply meant up to ten men could come in on those evenings to spar with opponents. It was a good way to gauge the skill of their private clients and perhaps find raw talent to further train for professional matches.

If a boxer wished to fight for the Stapleton salon, and he won a professional bout, that fighter would win fifty percent of the prize purse with the rest going into the Stapleton coffers. They would lend their notoriety while the fighter would lend his skill. It was a winning solution to both parties.

Beyond that, Lewis and his brothers had plans to perhaps offer boxing lessons in private homes once the salon turned a profit.

Their business venture had been open for a couple of weeks and though they currently had only a handful of signed clients, he was confident they would steadily grow. Already Duncan had made some meaningful connections. It was only a matter of time before men interested in indulging in the sport would make appointments.

Though it was two o'clock in the afternoon, there was only one client in the salon. The man, perhaps in his late twenties, was working with Alexander at one of the punching bags. Needing something to do, Lewis made his way into the office merely to stare out the window that overlooked the narrow, shadowed alley between this building and the next. He'd promised his mother that he would attend a rout tonight with her, for she wished to introduce him to the daughter of one of her friends. He'd only agreed to the scheme to circumvent the friction that would have come from outright refusing.

After all, there would be free brandy and perhaps food.

As he watched, a young man came into the alley. After looking furtively over his shoulder as if someone were following him, he prowled along the street, glancing to and fro, the upper portion of his face obscured by a slouch style cap. Then Lewis lost sight of him as he moved onto Brook Street itself.

Just as he was about to seat himself behind the desk, movement from the corner of his eye made him glance up and through the windows separating his office from the salon itself. The door from the narrow wooden staircase opened and the same young man that he'd seen in the alley stood there, peering about the room with shock and confusion in his expression.

How very odd. Perhaps a potential client?

When he looked at his brother, Alexander frowned and shrugged. Lewis nodded and lifted a hand in acknowledgement. He came around his desk and then moved out of his office and into the salon. As it appeared the young man might bolt, he hailed the newcomer.

"Welcome to Stapleton Boxing Salon. Is there something I can help you with?" The closer he came to the young man, the more clues became evident. Random dog hairs clung to the tweed jacket the boy wore that was much too heavy for the June warmth, and the sleeves were too long besides. Peaks of blonde hair were evident beneath the wool cap, but it was the large blue eyes that arrested Lewis' movement and had confusion gripping his mind.

"Uh…" The young man glanced around the room. "I, um, I would like to learn how to box, to fight," he said in a low voice that was either graveled with emotion, or raspy due to sickness, or some other anomaly meant to disguise said voice.

"We can certainly do that. If you'll follow me into my office, I can then take down specifics and find out how we can meet your needs." With that, he led the younger man through the salon and then into his office. "Please, feel free to sit." As he indicated one of the high-backed wooden chairs that faced the desk, he once more went behind that piece of furniture and sank onto the worn leather of the chair. It had come over from his study at home. "Perhaps you should tell me a bit about yourself."

"Right." The other man nodded. His gaze went to the window behind Lewis' chair, then darted toward the door that led into the salon. "My name is…" He cleared his throat. "Uh, my name is Nathan… Feathers."

"I see." Nathan Feathers. And was said as if being made up upon the spot. Lewis took a pen in hand, dipped the nub into the inkwell, and then began scribbling some notes. "Well, Mr. Feathers, how old are you?"

"Twenty-seven. Small for my age, I suppose."

"How did you hear about the salon?"

As the other man spoke, Lewis took a few notes while he covertly studied the newcomer. Quite short, he probably didn't top a couple of inches over five feet. Pale, smooth skin spoke to a middle to upper class life and not one that labored in the elements. The tweed jacket and waistcoat beneath went a long way into hiding full breasts, but wouldn't do if someone were to stare too closely. Long blonde lashes framed the almost impossibly blue eyes, but it was the pink lips and the dainty Cupid's Bow of the mouth that gave the secret away. If this person was a male, then he—Lewis—was a donkey. She might have fooled others on the street, but it didn't take much scrutiny to see that her disguise wasn't all that effective.

At least not in front of him.

The question now remained: why the devil was a woman here, and what should he do about the potential scandal?

"I beg your pardon, did you say you had encountered a bully recently?" That part of her story, at least, had penetrated his brain.

"Yes." The woman in disguise nodded. "At the docks."

What the deuce was a woman doing at the docks regularly, outside of making a living on her back? And this one didn't have such an air about her. Again, he studied her, tried to imagine what her form would appear like without being hidden by a young man's clothing. The curve of her breasts was quite the giveaway, and even if she'd wrapped them and somehow bound them with fabric, the longer he stared, the more he saw the womanly curves. She certainly wasn't a slim miss by any stretch, but pleasantly plump; she would no doubt be quite eye-catching in a gown beneath candlelight.

"What sort of unwanted attentions are you referring to?" Besides wanting to know more about her life, he needed to understand how best to help her should he decide to keep her on and actually give her lessons.

She briefly held her bottom lip between her teeth. No doubt it was an unconscious move, and she probably wasn't aware of it. "I am constantly being followed and harassed. Sometimes subjected to unwanted touches." Her voice lowered, and by this time, she'd apparently forgotten to disguise her voice. "Having unwanted kisses forced upon me, by a great beast of a man," she went on to say while keeping her gaze focused on his inkwell. "It is becoming a concerning problem."

"I see." Every word out of her mouth combined with the disguise furthered the intrigue surrounding her. Clearly, she needed boxing lessons for self-defense, but what was her daily life that she thought things had come to this? These were only two questions he needed to find the answers to. "Is anyone else in your family being picked on by this man?"

She gave a curt nod. "I have an eleven-year-old brother. It is my fear that he will be this man's next target if I don't submit to his demands."

Ah, now they were discovering the meat of the matter. "Where is this unwanted attention happening?"

"The East India Docks."

Why the devil did she ever have cause to be there? With every word she spoke, he grew more curious and concerned. "I beg your pardon, but what business do you have in that area of London?"

Her lips pulled downward into a frown, and from the way they curved and how the expression shifted on her rounded face, only a nodcock could believe she was a man. "My father owns a shipping and import business there. I do the books for him."

Fair enough. "Does your family live there?" If so, the danger would increase exponentially.

"We used to, but when my mother died and Papa's business became more lucrative, he decided to buy a modest townhouse in Mayfair. In Manchester Square. Thankfully, it is a quiet neighborhood with lush gardens, but..."

"But you are concerned this man of questionable morals might follow you there," Lewis finished for her in an equally low voice.

"Yes." When she finally raised her gaze to his, he bit back a gasp, for those blue pools were all too inviting as they reflected vulnerability and a trace of fear. "That is why I came here. I saw the lettering being painted on the windows last month. I thought that if I could learn how to fight, I might have a chance at defending myself."

"A noble pursuit, surely." With one huge difficulty. The young man was definitely *not* male. They couldn't exactly have a female in the salon. Not only would it provoke unwelcome questions, but the scandal and wagging tongues would bury their fledgling business before it even got started. "Bare knuckle boxing and fisticuffs is a highly physical sport. It requires endurance and close contact with one's opponent." To say nothing of an innate trust in oneself. The woman was so petite, she would easily be overpowered by any of the clients they'd already signed. Also, women could be more delicate and didn't tend to develop muscle mass as quickly as men.

This is a terrible idea. Intriguing, but terrible.

"I am well aware of that and will do whatever it takes."

For long moments, he rested his gaze on her, assessing the possibilities. How the devil would he even do such a thing, for at the heart of the matter, she was a female, and if he couldn't ensure her safety while out in the salon with other men, this would never work.

Besides, wouldn't he need to ask his brothers their opinion?

Tentatively, he would move forward, for the fear she felt, the fear that had motivated her to even come into the salon was quite real. "Well, I am the Earl of Lethbridge, but here I am Lewis Stapleton, part owner of this establishment. My two brothers are also here as instructors and owners. We offer private lessons three days a week with one day as an open bout class wherein all our students, as well as folks wishing to try the salon, can drop by to fight bouts with each other. Is this something you might find of interest?"

If possible, her face went even more pale than it already was. "It is going to have to be. I have no other choice." When she raised her gaze, she tugged at the brim of her cap to keep it shading part of her face. How anyone could think she was a young man was beyond his ken. "I grow weary of being attacked on a near daily basis. Even now, it terrifies me to know that I still have a job to do at my father's office, but when I go there, at some point, I will be molested."

If she were a man, the admission would have been concerning enough, but since she was a woman in disguise, his chest tightened with apprehension for her, and that made him curious. About both her and his reaction to this stranger.

"All right. Let me speak with my brother for a moment, then I will come back to you." As he spoke, Lewis rose from his chair and moved around the side of the desk. "I shouldn't be long."

As he exited the office, he pulled the door closed behind him. Then he sought out Alexander, made eye contact with him. "I would like a word, please," he said in low voice.

"Is this going to be another of your lectures on how you

know best?" He made an excuse to the man who currently punched at a sandbag, then led Lewis over to the fall wall where they could have relative privacy. "What is it?"

"Do you see the young man in the office?" When his brother glanced that way, he nodded. "I suspect that is a woman in disguise. There is something about her eyes that makes me think she is, in fact, not a man. There are other things there, as well, but that is beside the point. Regardless, she is frightened, and she wants boxing lessons so she can defend herself against an attacker."

"While I can understand that, her gender presents a unique problem for this salon." Alexander frowned as he continued to stare in the direction of the office. "You already know this."

"I do. However, is the greater crime not teaching her the skills she'll need to no doubt survive out there on her own?" If he turned her away today, would the next time she came into contact with her attacker be the last? How could he live with himself after that?

"Never say you've been a victim of a pair of pretty eyes."

"Come off it, man. This is a serious question." Lewis frowned and crossed his arms at his chest. "What should I do?"

"Is she willing to pay full price for lessons?"

He shrugged. "I haven't gotten to that part of the interview."

"Then you must have been distracted, hmm, when coin isn't uppermost in your mind?" When Lewis didn't answer, his brother continued. "If you do wish to teach her a few survival skills, how would that be possible? We simply can't have women in the salon."

"I am aware of that, but I could privately teach her in the office. We installed Venetian blinds at the windows in any event, and if we closed them, she would effectively be hidden from view of the salon." It had been one of the features they'd had installed on all the windows of the salon, not only to keep the harsh afternoon sun out but also to provide another layer of privacy for lessons during the evening hours.

He mused on how Venetian blinds may have originated in Persia, not the canal city of Venice, Italy; the origins of slatted blinds had existed for centuries. Ancient Egyptians tied reeds together to use as a window covering, and the Chinese used bamboo strips in the same way. The first examples of such were from around 1760—early Venetian blinds were made of two-inch wood slats hanging along cloth ribbons.

"God, you and the Venetian blinds." Alexander chuckled, but then he slowly nodded. "It could work, though. At least for today's lesson. Subsequent ones can be either early in the morning or in the evening after hours to keep her identity hidden."

"You wouldn't mind?" The more Lewis thought about it, the more the scenario began to take shape.

"Mind? Not while she's a paying customer." His brother shrugged again. "I won't begrudge anyone the ability to defend themselves, but I will caution you to be careful and to not get involved over and above what happens here in this salon. We have our own problems and don't need to take on anyone else's."

"I am not that man, and you know it." Though he did have his charitable causes he championed, he had never been in the habit of involving himself in the affairs of others. "Very well. I'll tell her the cost of each lesson and go from there."

Alexander nodded. "Go carefully. This could explode in our faces, and we have worked too hard to get the salon running."

"Agreed." With a nod at his brother, Lewis returned to the office and once more closed the door behind them, which caused the woman on the chair to startle. Then he manipulated the Venetian blinds, slowly closing them to block the view from the salon. "All right, Mr. Feathers, my brother and I are in agreement. We'll take you on as a client. Each lesson costs two pounds each. It sounds steep, but you can use these lessons over a lifetime."

"I can pay it." The woman in disguise reached into the pocket of her waistcoat and withdrew the necessary coins, leaned forward, and then laid them on the desktop. "When shall we begin?"

"Soon, of course."

"I would enjoy that immensely." Slowly, the faux Mr. Feathers stood, came into a clear space within the office.

He gestured to where she needed to stand and tried to curb his curiosity. "Once you've mastered the basic fighting techniques, we'll begin sparring practice." In her case, it would be in Hyde Park, early enough to provide privacy instead of in the salon.

"All right." Her eyes rounded. "You won't... injure me, will you?" Once more, her voice was graveled as one of her hands crept to her neck. "I couldn't begin to explain the bruises to my father or brother."

The fear in her expression tugged at his chest. "No, I won't. In fact, this first lesson, you and I won't share punches." What was her life like that fear always lurked in the backs of those bluer-than-blue eyes? Had she ever known happiness? "Let's get to it."

Mr. Feathers nodded. "What would you have me do?"

"Best to remove the jacket for better range of motion."

Once she took the garment off, Lewis fought to keep his expression passive. *Bloody hell.* How did she think he'd think she was a man? The buff-colored men's breeches, a linen shirt, and the waistcoat over the top of that that did nothing to hide her natural curves; he had difficulties maintaining concentration. Scuffed and worn Hessian-style boots—had she borrowed them from her brother?—completed the ensemble.

"Now what?"

"Uh..." Lewis resisted the urge to pull at his suddenly tight cravat. Dear God, those legs! His gaze went on a leisurely trip down the length of her body to pause at the tempting vee of her thighs. He took a ragged breath and firmly pinned his regard to her face, where indecision brewed. The disguise would fool no one... unless they weren't paying attention. "Fighting is easier without extra clothing. Here at the salon and in the ring, we box bare-chested and sometimes bare footed for that reason." But during public bouts, the crowd enjoyed seeing a well-worked physique.

Panic joined the fear in her expression. "I won't need to take my shirt off, will I?"

He understood her concern. "You will not." But she would need to be the one to admit to her gender. In the meanwhile, he would keep her secret. Shoving the fetching image of her in breeches from his mind, Lewis nodded. "I will write up a contract for my teaching services. It lists the payment amount per week. You can sign before you go today since you have already made the first deposit."

"Thank you." Mr. Feathers—for lack of a better moniker—stood with several feet of space between them, her posture stiff. No doubt she was ready to run.

After removing his own jacket, he tossed it across his desk. "Let's begin." Lewis closed the distance. "You need to learn how to make a proper fist." He held up a hand, fingers curled, thumb across his digits.

She experimented with her own fingers. "Like this?"

"No. Mind your thumb. It's too easy to break if tucked under." Again, he held up his own fist as he drifted to her side. A slight intake of breath betrayed her unease at his proximity, and that didn't sound like a man. Had she forgotten her disguise already? "There you go. Just like that." He nodded, and relief broke over her brow. "Now, let's work on your stance. Plant your feet, knees slightly bent, arms up and fists at the ready." He demonstrated the correct form. "The fists are what connect to your opponent, but your arm is where the power lies. As Gentleman Jackson says, you'll make more of an impact with a well-timed blow than using your body as a battering ram."

His father had employed a mixture of that man's methods with many of his own, and that was how Lewis taught the discipline.

Awkwardly, she assumed the position. "How do you know

which fist to punch with and when? It seems overwhelming to me."

"All that will come in time. Right now, I'm only concerned with the basics." He demonstrated how to throw a punch. "Lead with your first two knuckles. Where they go is where your fist will land."

"Ah." She moved her fist but twisted her arm slightly in the process.

"Let me show you." He maneuvered himself behind her. The faint scent of violets drifted to his nose—another mistake in assuming the disguise. "Straighten your arm when you swing." He framed her body with his, leading her arm like how it should be if she were punching on her own, but her whole being stiffened, the muscles tensing as if she would dart from the room. "You must relax. Boxing while stressed will injure you."

What the devil was she enduring in her home life that led her to be so on edge?

"Sorry." The woman flinched when his head came too close to hers. She shied away from him and spun about, facing him with alarm in her expression and fear in her eyes. Her pulse beat fast in her neck while her chest heaved. "It will take some time for me to be at ease with all of this."

"Or with me as your teacher," he added in a soft voice. When she gave him a tight nod, he sighed. Obviously, he had a different sort of fight ahead and needed to address her fear before moving forward. "Boxing is a sport of gentlemen."

"I shall be the judge of that." Was she even aware her voice had changed, and she talked as she probably was in real life?

"It is a sport of control. Gentlemen don't fight to kill or intimidate." When she remained silent, he stifled the urge to sigh again. *Slowly, Lewis. Go slowly.* "You have my promise that I won't hurt you; I want you to learn self-defense as much as you do."

She nodded, but the fear didn't leave her eyes. "Thank you."

"However, you will need to work *with* me. In doing this, you'll learn trust and courage." When she eyed him with trepidation, he sighed. "In order to do that, feel the fear, defy it, and go forward anyway." He made certain to modulate his voice into soothing tones. "Boxing will give you the confidence you seek, and it will make you stronger. In that, I speak from experience."

"You were once pestered by a bully?"

"No, but I have two brothers. Also, my father was a prize fighter of some acclaim… and I was a bit of a problem at times at university."

They both shared a laugh.

He gestured to his side. "Would you like to try again? My promise stands."

"I…" When her eyes darted to the door, he stifled a sigh. "I'm sure I'm a disappointment for a man, but I don't trust other men immediately."

"Understandable." How long did she hope to perpetuate her disguise? He suddenly wanted to be the one she could count on. "I'm going to teach you everything you need to know about boxing and defense, yet trust *must* be present." He held up his hands, palms out. "I mean no harm."

One corner of her lips quirked with the beginnings of a smile. It fascinated him. What would it take for her to grin in genuine pleasure? "I am trying my best, Mr. Stapleton."

"Good." Yes, damn it, he was a gentleman, and that meant keeping her a student in his mind, no matter that her subtle floral scent teased his senses and her scandalously clad form distracted him. "Now, assume the stance. If I touch you, it's to correct your posture, not for a nefarious purpose."

"I appreciate your willingness to teach me despite my reticence." Though her smile was slight and tremulous, he relaxed.

"As with any relationship, we will go slowly until we are able to move around each other seamlessly." And devil take it all, he couldn't wait to delve into the mystery of her past as well as her home life.

Chapter Four

June 20, 1817
Dawson's Imports
Robinhood Lane
East India Dock
London, England

CECILIA GLANCED THIS way and that as she trod over the boardwalk. Of course, it just had to rain today, when she was already running late getting into her father's office. Ever since her introductory boxing lesson two days ago, she'd been exhausted from the unaccustomed exercise, and some of her muscles ached where she didn't expect, but at least it was a step in the right direction.

Oddly enough, she couldn't wait for her next lesson, which was scheduled for later this afternoon.

Of course, part of that excitement could be to see the earl again. She couldn't be certain, but he might already know that she'd been a woman in disguise. Though he hadn't let on that he knew, he'd treated her with kindness and respect. Would he have done the same with a man? Since she didn't know him at all, it was difficult to tell, but he possessed the most beautiful pair of eyes she'd ever seen. At the outset, the depths were hazel, but in the sunlight which had streamed through the rear window in his office, they had changed to a rich brown with golden flecks. And he'd smelled so good! Cedarwood, orange, with a slight hint of leather that she could still discern in her nose two days later.

Stop daydreaming, Ceci. It's unbecoming, and you're not looking for romance besides.

Not that anything would ever happen between them. He was an earl for goodness sake, and she was naught but a captain's daughter, and him a merchant at that. Titled men didn't dally with the daughters of cits. Everyone knew that. However, he'd been the first man to treat her with respect instead of a potential bed partner.

Of course, she'd been disguised as a young man, so there was that.

So lost in thought was she that when Mr. Derrickson approached her not far from her father's shipping office, she wasn't aware that he'd crept up on her. By the time she realized the danger she was in, it was too late.

With a gasp, Cecilia came to a halt just before she would have run bodily into the mountain of a man. "I am running late and not inclined to entertain your idiotic notions today," she told him as a warning and tried to look as menacing as she could.

"Don't be like that, Miss Dawson. I only bother you because I fancy you." With a crooked grin, he stepped into her path.

"That is all well and good, but I do not return your feelings." Though she had to tip her head up in order to peer into his face— he was a good foot taller than she—she was forced to put a hand to shield her face from the rain, for the shallow brim of her bonnet didn't help. "Now, let me pass." Could she remember all she'd learned from that one brief boxing lesson?

"Not until you promise to be my wife."

She snorted. "I would need to be dead for several days before that would ever happen."

"Then you haven't thought hard enough about being with me." He had the audacity to wrap a beefy hand around her upper arm. "One night in my bed will have you begging me to marry you."

Good lord. What a nodcock.

"I rather doubt that." When she made a move to go around him, he propelled her backward and into the shadows from one of the warehouses. "Unhand me."

"Not till I get that kiss." And his big face came toward hers.

Why were men so annoying, and beyond that, dangerous? Well, she was tired of being treated like an object, as if she had no other value in this world beyond being someone's bedmate or a way to stem frustration.

"Let me go." When the man forced one of her arms behind her back, pain skittered down that limb. Fear twisted down her spine, and as she tried to jam a knee between his legs, he dodged away from her.

"None of that this time."

Remembering what Mr. Stapleton had taught her about forming a fist, she curled her fingers into one like he'd instructed. She didn't hold much confidence in her ability to take down an attacker right now, but she had to try something. Then she pulled back her fist, let it fly into what she thought was a weak upper-cut—wasn't that what he'd called it?—and then bit back a crow of victory when Mr. Derrickson stumbled back after her fist connected with his jaw. However, connecting a fist with anything that solid meant there was a bit of pain in her hand.

"That is no way to treat your future husband." The man retaliated by swinging out a meaty hand and slapped her across the cheek. "I'll beat that spirit out of you."

Pain exploded at the side of her head. From the force of a blow, she fell to the boardwalk while he towered over her. As she cowered and steeled herself for the next contact—for she well remembered what came next from her failed engagement—her father ran over to them at that point.

"How dare you lay hands on my daughter." Immediately, he laid into Mr. Derrickson, grabbed him by the collar, and spun him around. He landed a punch to the man's jaw. "If I see you around here again, you'll get worse than this." Once more taking hold of the back of the bigger man's jacket, he shuttled him across the boardwalk, then pitched him into the harbor.

Masculine laughter followed the incident, for workers around the dock had born witness to the debacle. They scattered when her father glanced their way, though.

"Are you hurt?" he asked as he helped Cecilia to her feet.

"I have been through worse." Though tears stung her eyes, she blinked away the urge to cry because it could have gone much more drastically. "Every time I am out here, Mr. Derrickson thinks to bother me, and after today, I don't know how I'm going to survive it."

"You shouldn't come out there any longer," her father said as he escorted her into the shipping office. "I let you do the books against my better judgment, but obviously, it is too dangerous for you here."

She shook her head. "What would I do at home? Sit around and work embroidery? You know I am not skilled at that."

"Something must be done." After he'd guided her to one of the chairs in front of his desk, he leaned a hip against that piece of furniture and crossed his arms at his chest. A fierce frown followed. "I had no idea you were being harassed. How long?"

Cecilia shrugged. "At least a few months." She touched the fingertips of one hand to the side of her face where she'd been hit. The skin was tender but not broken. Perhaps it was time for her to confess all to him. "In fact, being bothered on a regular basis, I made the decision to take boxing lessons."

"I beg your pardon?"

"I paid for a lesson in fisticuffs and had it two days ago. It was brief and I was dressed as a boy, but though I was a bit frightened, I think it will prove helpful."

Her father's eyebrows rose in surprise. "You are taking boxing lessons." It wasn't a question. "And you were disguised as a boy?"

"I borrowed some of James' clothes. The sleeves of the shirt and jacket were too long and the boots slightly too big, but it did the job." She sighed. "I rather doubt I would have been allowed into the boxing salon otherwise. To be fair, the owner of the establishment took me into his office where it was more private, and that was where we had our first lesson."

For the first time, she gave thought to the consequences of what she'd done. She had been alone with a man, and if he had known she was a woman, did that constitute being compromised? It was too difficult to tell. Did it matter so much since she wasn't part of the *beau monde*? Again, the line was blurry.

"You visited a boxing salon of your own accord."

"Yes."

He nodded. Admiration shone in his eyes. "I'm proud of you, but going in disguise was a mistake. I mean, I understand why; you needed to protect your reputation, but it was still a mistake."

"Why?" She frowned, not following his logic.

"Because, when you are accosted by the dock workers or fishermen, you are in skirts. You need to learn how to move and dart about while in your ordinary clothing instead of breeches. You'll never be dressed like a boy when molested."

"Oh!" That made sense. "Thank you for that. I'd never thought of it in such a way before." Slowly, she nodded. "I'll tell Lord Lethbridge today of my real identity when I go for my second lesson."

"What?" He gawked at her. "The Earl of Lethbridge is your boxing instructor?" Incredulity rang in his voice.

"Yes." One of her eyebrows rose. "Do you know him?"

"I knew his father. He was a premier bare-knuckle boxer. Won several bouts in his time as well as brought in big prize purses." He shrugged. "A pity he died from the sport."

"I didn't know that." For long moments, she stared at her parent. "No wonder the earl was so standoffish outside of giving me instructions regarding the lesson."

"Well, according to gossip, the earl's father's death was abrupt and unexpected. The oldest son wasn't expecting to take the title yet. Been about two years or so since he did."

"I'm sorry to hear that. He must be devastated." Cecilia frowned, for she would always carry the grief of losing her mother with her. "I'll give him my condolences this afternoon."

"You will still attend the lesson after what happened?"

"Why not? It's even more needed now." A long-suffering breath escaped her. "I grow weary of always needing to stay aware, of never having the freedom to walk to this office without being harassed, never being taken seriously because I'm a woman."

He unbent enough to lean over and buss her cheek. "I can't guess how difficult this is for you, but I will ask that you not come here alone. Bring a footman or wait until I'm available. Otherwise, I can bring the paperwork and books home for you to work on there."

"Perhaps that is best until I have built up confidence and skill in boxing." When her father didn't appear convinced, she sighed and gained her feet. "I can do this, Papa. I can. What's more, the whole sport of boxing is interesting. I'd like to learn more." She kept her thoughts regarding the earl to herself. "And if I can learn how to successfully defend myself, where is the harm?"

"I want to keep you safe, Ceci. If your reputation is damaged because of this, there will be nothing I can do. You won't be able to make a good match." Concern creased his brow. "While I'll let you have a bit of independence, you must understand that I will do everything I can to keep you safe."

"I know." She took his hand, squeezed his fingers. "Thank you, but I also need to do this on my own."

I refuse to be one of those women who becomes a victim because she thinks she should take the abuse.

ONCE MORE SHE found herself inside the private office of Lewis Stapleton, and for the past half hour, she'd been punching his raised hands, but it was awkward to gauge distance, for he'd encouraged her to wear a pair of padded leather mittens to avoid busting up her knuckles. Now, he was instructing how to block blows as he struck out with his hands, also in mittens.

And she was failing at this simple task, for all she could see in her mind's eye was Mr. Derrickson coming at her, swinging his beefy hand.

"Hold." With a huff, he held up a hand. "You are distracted." It wasn't a question.

"I am. Sorry." She frowned and rested her mitten-covered hands on her hips. As of yet, she hadn't told him of her true gender.

He yanked off a mitten. "Because of this?" When he brushed his fingertips along the slope of the cheek that had been slapped two days ago, she trembled.

"Yes." She could scarcely breathe with him in such close proximity. His hands, so rough and powerful enough to throw punches, were also gentle and as delicate as angel's wings when he caressed her cheek. Yet he remained reticent, focused. "It isn't as bad as it looks. Faint bruising."

"Who did this to you?" He snapped his teeth together. When she shook his head, he sighed. "What aren't you telling me?"

It was now or never. "I have come here under false pretenses, which rolls right into the reason I'm here at all." Watching him the whole time, Cecilia removed her slouch-style cap. As his gaze went to her tightly bound hair, she said, "I am a woman. My name is Miss Cecilia Dawson, not Mr. Feathers, but when I said I was being bullied at the docks, that was true. One of the men there hit me two days ago."

The earl's nod was curt. "I'm glad you told me the truth, for I suspected you weren't a young man almost immediately."

"Oh." That sapped at her newly built confidence. "The man trapped me, wrenched one of my arms behind my back. I attempted to fight him like you've showed me during our first lesson, but then my father came and intervened. Pitched the man into the harbor."

A muscle in the earl's cheek ticced. "Men who hit women are the worst sort of scum." The deceptively quiet, warning rumble in his voice sent gooseflesh sailing over her arms.

Cecilia ignored his response, for if she didn't, she would break into tears, and she wanted to appear strong in Mr. Stapleton's eyes. "He is a brute, but he's stubborn and will try again. That or—"

"Or?" He looked sharply at her.

"Or I'm not a good enough student. I should have been able to rout him."

Mr. Stapleton jerked on the padded glove he'd just removed, yanked the ties with his teeth. "Or I'm a miserable teacher." The annoyance had grown in his tone, but this time it was directed at himself.

The tautness across her hands from the mittens' laces reminded her why she was here. "You are a brilliant teacher. I wish we had more time together than one hour for lessons."

"Why?"

She shrugged. "To talk?"

He snorted. "I am not much for talking." The despair in his eyes was genuine. What demons did he wrestle with? "I'd like to hope our lessons are helping you."

"It is early days, and there is still much I need to learn." Cecilia cut the air with a padded mitten. She stared at him. "You've said yourself that going against better opponents helps you grow. Here's your chance. Show me."

A grudging grin tipped the corners of his lips. Flutters moved through her belly. "Are you trying to boost my ego, Miss Dawson?"

"Either that or move your arse into fighting with me." She smacked her gloved hands together. "After all, I have paid for this lesson."

"Fair enough. And direct. I appreciate that." He chuckled. "Let me show you a choke hold for those times your tormentor is persistent."

"How—" Before she could finish the question, he darted behind her, wrapped one arm about her middle, which rendered her arm immobile, while his other arm went around her neck with her throat in the vee of the bent elbow. "Mr. Stapleton?" A trace of fear climbed her spine, but she knew he wouldn't hurt her. He wasn't that sort of man.

But men were also liars.

"The trick is to squeeze just enough to cut off the airflow, but only as a last resort, for it's all too easy to kill." His voice in her ear was both comforting and alarming. "Once you cross over into that territory, you'll be forever changed."

She clawed at his arm, but her mittens made that ineffective. Her pulse increased into a frantic rhythm. "Let me go." Panic filled her chest. Had she put her trust in the wrong man?

"I know it's uncomfortable, but this *can* save your life," he said into her ear, breaking through the haze of anxiety. "You can either apply pressure like this." He tightened his arm for a fraction of a second but then relaxed his hold. "Or move your forearm to his throat, Lia. Like so." He demonstrated the technique. "Secure that arm with your other one. It's your choice how you go about it, but surprise is the key. If you must jump upon his back in order to do this since you are petite, do it."

When he released her, Cecilia gulped in a breath, and then annoyance roared into her chest. She rounded on him, getting off a punch that landed square into his shoulder. "Never do that to me again without warning, lesson or not." It didn't matter that she rather liked the shortened version of her name he'd used.

"My apologies." Mr. Stapleton stepped backward, his hands raised. "I want you to be fully prepared."

"Noted." She threw another punch but missed him. His return volley bussed her cheek. "Arse." Another one of her swings connected with his glove, but the rest missed. She blew out a frustrated breath. "It's not working."

"Because you are still distracted." Mr. Stapleton dropped his hands. "What makes you angry, sad, frustrated? Use those emotions. Channel them and let them fuel you. At times of crisis, they might be the only things that help you focus."

"Is that what you do during a prize fight?"

"At times."

How fascinating. "Does it help after the match is over?"

"Not always, but that's where your power lies. Take it back. Stop letting men steal it. Use *your* power and fight for what *you* want." The encouragement in his voice soothed the tangle of her emotions.

"Right." Cecilia launched herself at him. She got off an uppercut to his chin but missed the second time. He returned with punches of his own, tagging both her cheeks.

"Damn your eyes, Mr. Stapleton," she hissed, as her ire with herself grew.

"Keep going." He circled her. Sweat trickled from one temple. "Flow into the rhythm of the fight. This is only your second lesson."

She threw a punch again. This time she connected with his flat abdomen. Part of her mind wondered what he looked like *sans* shirt.

He retreated with a faint grin. "Impressive." As blows were exchanged and the slap of leather on leather blended with their grunts and throaty utterances, he talked to her. "Has your attacker come after your brother?"

"Not that I know of." One of her gloves slid over his cheek.

"Good. If he is ever accosted, feel free to bring him here." He ducked her next punch. "No one should feel threatened."

"Agreed, but when one doesn't have a title behind them, one is often the prey." The exercise left her panting with sweat sticking the shirt to her back.

"Sometimes that is the reason, but it is also strength, how you carry yourself. Predators are naught but bullies who will usually back down if you fight back." Mr. Stapleton tagged a glove into her midsection. He grunted when she gasped. "But you are a quick study, and you are short. That gives you an advantage. *You* decide if you are prey."

Cecilia gave him a tight grin. "It is difficult."

"Indeed, but you *can* do this. Get mean if you must, and throw the rules away if it helps. When survival is in the offing, nothing else matters."

Truly, he was so different than other men that it was laughable. "I'll remember that." Her footwork was nearly as good as Mr. Stapleton's—or he was humoring her—for now it was he who struggled to match her movements.

"Keep going." A muscle ticced in his jaw.

"It is more work than I anticipated."

"Anything worth having is."

Cecilia tried an uppercut, but Mr. Stapleton bounded away, and the tip of her glove glanced along his jaw. "Your father taught you how to box." It wasn't a question.

"Yes."

"Were you bullied at school?"

Shock lined his face and reflected in his eyes. "How could you know that? Not even my brothers know."

Well, good for me. Her next swing caught him square on the jaw. Cecilia snickered at the surprise in his expression. "I have listened to what you won't tell me. And no doubt you wanted to impress your father, the prize fighter, gain his attention... for you felt you failed at training to be his heir."

Was her guess correct?

Mr. Stapleton rolled his shoulders. "I thought I was better at keeping things close." He drilled a fist into one of her palms.

That connection and the power behind it sent her back a step. It also had awareness of him flaring into every nerve ending. "We are all broken in some way, and some of us just pay more attention to the silences... because we've had to." She shrugged. If she had listened more to her fiancé, perhaps things would have been different for her now.

"Meaning?" Frown lines creased his forehead.

"Second guessing what men really mean grows more annoying each year." A trace of bitterness clung to her words. She used that emotion to throw her next punch, which connected soundly with his glove. "I detest being seen as only a bedmate, something to be used and then discarded."

"Understandable, and the punch was impressive."

"Thank you." She threw another punch. The satisfying slap of leather met her ears. "I'm enjoying this lesson more than the first."

"You've a natural talent." Mr. Stapleton's stance relaxed slightly.

Cecilia took the opportunity to swing again. This time, her punch connected solidly to his cheek with enough force to spin him about. She giggled. "I guess I did need to channel that anger."

"You've done well." Pride reflected in his eyes.

She beamed. "See? You *are* a great teacher."

"But remember, there are times when going blindly, led by emotion, will hurt rather than help." But the corners of his mouth tipped in a grin.

"I'll bear that in mind." Cecilia's spirits and confidence soared. It was an extraordinary feeling. "Boxing has changed everything. Thank you!" So exuberant was she that Cecilia threw herself into his arms.

"Argh!" The force of her movement sent him off-balance, and he staggered backward but never recovered. They tumbled to the floor and onto a straw-filled pallet. "Oomph." He landed heavily on his back and she on top of him, more or less straddling his waist, one padded mitten resting on his heaving chest.

"Oh." Her attitude subtly changed as she stared down into his face from her new perch. He was so solid; the heat of him seeped through her thin breeches to warm her legs. And she felt… powerful in this position. Her pulse accelerated.

Mr. Stapleton watched her. Slowly, he tugged off one of his padded mittens and then the other, tossing them toward his desk. "Cecilia?" Unnamed emotion graveled that one word.

"Hmm?" Her throat went dry. Never in the whole of her

engaged life had she been given the chance to straddle a man, let alone ride him during the one coupling she'd had.

His body tensed. "This is highly scandalous. If we're caught…"

"I care not for that." She rid herself of her padded mittens merely to run her palms up his chest. Tingles played up and down her spine. Slowly, she leaned down as warning bells clanged in her head and kept going until their lips almost touched. "Much." The risk to them both was great.

"What are you doing?" Gently, he held onto her forearms. His eyes darkened into a smoky green shade filled with the same need pulsing through her veins.

"I'm not sure," she whispered. Oh, he smelled so good. She breathed in at the same time he expelled breath. Literally, they shared the same air as she held his gaze. "Mr. Stapleton?"

"Yes?"

"May I kiss you?" Surely, she had gone mad.

"God, yes."

Cecilia stroked her fingers along his cheek. As her heart pounded, she closed the final few inches and kissed his lips.

A shuddering sigh escaped him, but he made no other sound. Nor did he move. Instead, he waited and watched her, letting her decide.

She appreciated the fact he gave her the lead, for it went a long way into building back her trust. While smoothing the hair back from his brow, she explored every inch of his lips. Oh, he was heavenly, both hard and soft at the same time, and the faint bitterness of brandy clung to his mouth. Perhaps he'd indulged in a glass before their lesson.

Eventually, she pulled a bit away but continued to peer at him while her heart trembled as if on the verge of flight, and need throbbed between her thighs. That reaction was something she'd not gotten from her fiancé. Was that odd? "That was…"

"Exactly." Mr. Stapleton slipped his palms up her arms, then the sides of her neck until he finally cupped her face between his hands. When she sighed, he kissed her back with more finesse and vigor than she'd given him. When he finished, he said, "Yes, it *was* that, exactly."

"I want you to know that I don't go around kissing strange men."

"I'll take your word for it; I don't know you that well. However, boxing is an intimate sport at times."

She smiled. "Should I let you up?"

Mischief sparkled in his eyes. "Unless you would like to continue kissing me."

Should she?

"We're already in a heap of scandal."

"There is that."

"Good." His whole body tensed as he wrapped his arms around her. Then he flipped them both over and pressed her into the pallet with his weight on top of her. "I suppose this is as good a way as any to know you better."

As he claimed her lips, Cecilia gave herself over to the experience. With her fingers buried in the hair at his nape, she encouraged him to kiss her soundly. Mr. Stapleton was an intelligent man, for he'd understood her message and teased the seam of her lips with the tip of his tongue. Oh, how utterly delicious that was! She gasped from the wonder of it, and when he slid that organ into her mouth to tangle with hers, she was lost on the heated sensations crashing into her.

For the first time in a long while, fear and worry had no hold over her. She held him in her arms and enjoyed each nuance of their embrace. When he shifted slightly, the insistent bulge of his arousal pressed into her thigh that was between his legs. She shivered in anticipation. What would coupling with this man of a hundred mysteries be like? Surely different than it had been with her fiancé. Mr. Stapleton respected her, supported her, encouraged her, and he certainly would never beat her. He genuinely wanted the best for her, and that meant... everything.

The heat filling her body was bigger than the obvious desire she had for him. As he kissed her, he held her closer, and in his arms she knew peace and protection... and she wanted it to continue.

But he wasn't hers; he was an earl as well as her boxing instructor, and this had been a temporary bout of insanity. In the process of trying to slide out from beneath him, Cecilia managed to dig her knee into the soft flesh between his legs.

"Damn." Immediately, he rolled off her, clutching his privates with one hand as she scrambled to her feet.

"I'm sorry." What a silly goose she was. "Are you hurt badly?" Seconds later, she kneeled beside him. "Can I call for assistance?" Truly, she didn't understand what to do if a man's member was injured.

"That was a mistake, Lia." He easily took hold of her and flipped them both over until he leaned over her, holding his weight off her body with his forearms.

"What?" Once more, her heart pounded, but not from fear.

"Never show compassion or concern for your opponent in the ring. It can prove deadly."

"But that is what makes a person human."

"When you are in the fight of your life, none of that matters. Your first and only responsibility is survival. Do you understand?"

"Yes." For long moments, she shared a stare with him, then he lifted off her, got to his feet, and helped her to stand. "Good. I'd say this second lesson has been quite successful."

Chapter Five

June 20, 1817
Stapleton Boxing Salon
Mayfair, London

IT HAD BEEN two days since Lewis had temporarily misplaced his sanity and had kissed Miss Dawson in this very room. Two days since she'd admitted she was a young woman in disguise. Two days since she'd knocked him on his arse with beginner's luck in swinging punches.

To be fair, he'd been distracted over her face and form, but that shouldn't have mattered. She was a student, and such a thing couldn't happen again.

Still, he couldn't evict the incident from his mind, and because of that, he had the devil's own time trying to sleep for the past two nights. The remembrance of her lips against his, the way her soft curves fit against his harder body, the sounds of pleasure she'd made when he'd kissed her, the way excitement and awe had shone in her blue eyes for the seconds she'd straddled him all worked to cloak the common sense he usually showed.

What the devil is wrong with me? Certainly, he'd known better than to even engage in such a scandalous activity, and with an innocent and a stranger to boot. *God, Lewis, get your head out of your arse and don't muck this venture up.* Distraction was much of the reason he'd fled to the boxing salon before it had officially opened for the day.

Unfortunately, his brothers apparently had the same idea, for they arrived at the salon a half hour after he had. He saw them as they entered the space from the windows in his office. With a sigh, he stood up from his desk and then joined them in the lesson space.

"What are the two of you doing here so early?"

Both brothers showed varying degrees of surprise upon seeing him.

It was Duncan who spoke first. "More to the point, what are you doing here? The last time I knew, you didn't rise from your bed until nearly noon."

"Ordinarily, that is true." Lewis shoved a hand through his hair before resting his hands on his hips. "However, I've been having trouble sleeping recently, and I haven't been to my club since we opened the salon. Too much to do."

Alexander narrowed his eyes. "While that may be so, there is something else at play here." As he spoke, his brother tidied the pallets and mattress ticks. "You have been acting oddly ever since you took on that new client, that young man, the short one."

"You're right," Duncan said with a nod. "As soon as that young man's first lesson was over, you were acting differently. In fact, why the devil would you conduct a private lesson behind closed blinds when he's no different than any of our other clients?"

Well, damn.

"There *is* something I haven't told you, something I only just recently found out," he admitted in a soft voice. Not understanding why this bothered him so much, Lewis leaned a shoulder against the wooden frame that held up one of the straw-filled bags.

"Shit, Lewis, have you mucked this up for us already?" Censure rang in Alexander's voice as he glared. "We haven't even been open a month."

"Come off it. Of course I didn't." Much. "Uh, when the

young man in question first approached me for lessons in boxing and self-defense, I was doubtful, for something didn't ring true about the fellow's appearance and demeanor."

Duncan frowned as he tidied the pile of padded mittens. "Meaning?"

Lewis blew out a breath. "I suspected the young Mr. Feathers was a woman in disguise but didn't push for the admission at that time."

Shock reflected on his middle brother's face. "Why not?"

He shrugged and then crossed his arms at his chest. "There was no need to tip her hand at that point. She was frightened and wary, nearly shrank away from me when I barely touched her to teach her the positions or how to form a fist."

Duncan came over with a bucket of dirty rags in his hand. "What happened then?"

"I honestly thought it might be a one-off experience because I wasn't certain she'd come back after the first lesson." He pushed off the wooden frame in favor of pacing the length of the salon floor. "Then, two days ago, she returned for her second lesson."

"Still disguised as a boy?" Duncan wanted to know.

"Yes." He nodded. "She paid the fee without complaint, wouldn't let me keep things at the basics, so I put her into some mittens and give her some pointers on sparring so she could get the feel of hitting her fists into something other than my hands."

Alexander nodded. "Good next step. She must either be a quick study or have some natural skill for you to move to mittens so soon."

"Honestly, I'm impressed." He shrugged again. "Truth to tell, she knocked me on my arse when she rushed me. I wasn't expecting it, and my knee decided to lock at the moment of impact, so I went down hard on my back."

Both of his brothers snickered.

Heat crept up the back of his neck. "She did well. Even admitted she was a woman and removed her cap so I could see her hair that had been pulled back into a severe bun." In his mind's eye, he saw the scene replay, felt the weight of her on top of him. "After that, things changed. The mood shifted."

"How?" Alexander asked as Duncan continued to gather dirtied rags from around the space. "Changed as in you told her you would cease her lessons since the truth came out?"

"Ah, no." Lewis shook his head. "I… uh…" He heaved out a huff. "I kissed the woman, or rather she kissed me, which I would never have expected given her wariness of men in general."

"I beg your pardon, but did you say that you kissed her? A woman you don't know? A veritable stranger you've met a grand total of two times?" Shock reflected on Alexander's face as he gawked at Lewis.

"Yes."

The same emotions lay stamped through Duncan's expression. "I never thought you had in in you, Lewis. Damn." A wide smile curved his lips. "How was she? From the looks of her in those breeches, she's got enough curves to tempt the saints."

Mild annoyance rose in his chest. His brother was a womanizer, and the last thing Miss Dawson needed was his kind of harassment. "Have some respect."

"Why? *You* obviously didn't if you kissed her." There was a challenge in Duncan's eyes as he stared Lewis down.

"I deserve that." Clearly, he'd gone mad in that moment. "It was a kiss, nothing more, and it won't happen again. You both have my promise." Had he become so randy from not having a woman in his life for a year that he'd kiss the first one he came by? God, what an idiot he was.

"I'm afraid I don't even know what to think." Alexander slowly shook his head. He darted his gaze between the brothers. "What do I do?"

"What the hell do you think? Tell her there is no possible way she can continue taking boxing lessons!" Alexander's voice rose with each word. "It's pure folly as well as scandal to have her continue to come here." He regarded Lewis as if he'd grown two heads. "If she talks about taking lessons, or hell, about you kissing her… can you imagine the scandal, not only for the salon but also for your personal life?"

Damn, but he hadn't given his life a thought. "I'll be honest, I'd only cared about the salon. However, Miss Dawson won't talk. She's not the type to blab for a sensation." Neither was she a fortune hunter. Frankly, he doubted that had ever occurred to her; she was only concerned about keeping herself safe.

Duncan snorted. "How do you know? You said yourself she's a stranger."

"I just know." He shrugged. "It's a feeling."

"It's shocking you're such a nodcock." Alexander shook his head. "What *do* you know of her? Other than wanting boxing lessons?"

He narrowed his eyes on his brother. Though their skepticism was valid, they should realize he wouldn't put his family or their business into jeopardy for the attentions of a woman—any woman. "Next to nothing except being harassed by a brutish man at the docks."

"Why the hell was she at the docks?"

"Apparently, she keeps the books for her father's shipping business. Other than that, I don't know if she lives there or how often she's at the office."

For long moments, his brothers stared at him.

Finally, Alexander nodded. "Perhaps you should start there."

"How?"

"What the hell do you mean *how*? You go be charming. Meet with her outside of the salon capacity, and you start asking questions, inquire into her life and past."

Lewis frowned. "What difference will that make? We don't do the same for any of our other clients."

"True, but then our other clients aren't female." One of Alex's eyebrows rose in challenge. "If she is adamant about pursuing lessons, something will need to be worked out. We can't have skirts trailing in here."

"I agree." His mind went in a thousand different directions.

Yet that fear in her eyes hadn't been false. She was truly worried.

Duncan cleared his throat. "Well, we did open the salon for people of all walks of life. We just didn't count on the fact that women might be interested. You could either give her private lessons or she could come here in disguise after hours." He shrugged. "But you never answered my earlier question."

"Oh? What?"

A cheeky expression went over his face. "Did you enjoy the kiss? You've had a bit of a dry run lately, and I find it more than interesting that you showed enough of an interest in a woman to kiss her, regardless of how it came about."

The heat on the back of his neck had returned, but he couldn't hold back his grin. "Oddly, I did, but it can't happen again. I can't afford the distraction."

And he hoped to God that would hold true.

WHEN MISS DAWSON arrived at the salon that afternoon, he ushered her into his office that already had the blinds closed, and ignored the curious look Alexander shot him. Though she was dressed once more as a young man, she removed the cap as soon as she dropped onto a low sofa at the rear of the room beneath the window that overlooked the alley.

"You seem quite harried, Miss Dawson. Is all well?" Though he'd only spent two hours in her company over the past four days, he'd looked forward to this visit.

"It is becoming more and more difficult to go by my father's shipping office due to the unwanted attentions of Mr. Derrickson." She tangled her gloved fingers together in her lap while her eyes held a sheen of tears. "I managed to evade him this afternoon, and only because one of his fellows called his attention away, but I can't speak to the future." Briefly, she bit her bottom lip. "I wished James was with me, but he is with his friends today."

He frowned. "James is your beau?"

"Of course not. Don't be silly." When her gaze snapped to his, an electric sort of sensation twisted down his spine. "He is my brother." With a sigh, she removed her gloves and then shoved them into a satchel she carried that showed the outline of a book or two. Perhaps she had visited the bookshop nearby. "In any event, I've looked forward to this lesson."

Finally, there was a natural break he needed. "About that." Unbidden, he sank onto the sofa a bit away from her. "We should use this time for a discussion instead of actually boxing work."

When her lips turned downward, he couldn't tear his gaze away from her mouth. "Whyever for?"

Pull yourself together, Stapleton!

"We were rather carried away at our last session, and I don't want there to be an excess of emotion this time around. Also, I do apologize for my conduct with the kiss. You can be assured that such will not happen again."

For long moments, she regarded him, her expression inscrutable. Then she nodded. "I agree. My behavior was unconscionable as well. Because of my forwardness, things bordered on the scandalous. I wasn't thinking." Then she dropped her gaze to her hands in her lap. "Does this mean you don't wish to give me boxing lessons any longer?"

"No!" He cleared his throat and tempered his enthusiastic reply. "That is, I would never begrudge anyone the chance to learn to defend themselves. However, surely you must know that now your secret is out, I can hardly have you here while other men are about, for I don't wish for you to think you need to continually hide in a disguise."

"What do you mean?" The inquiry was couched in a tremulous whisper that went straight through his chest.

Lewis held up a hand to stave off hysterics. "What I am proposing is this. We continue to have lessons, but they will either need to be here after hours, at your father's office, or at times in

Hyde Park where we would have more room to spar—during the non-busy times, of course."

"Truly?" When she raised her gaze to his once more, those blue pools of her eyes were so fathomless he wondered what it would feel like to drown in them.

"Of course." Mentally, he gave his head a shake. *Focus on the task at hand, man. Don't let her become a distraction. She is a student, nothing more.* "First, I would like to learn a bit more about you, if you are of a mind to share."

"All right." She nodded. "I promise to answer to the best of my abilities, but I should hope you will return the favor sometime."

"I will." Was that crossing the line of instructor and student? At the last second, he tamped down the urge to snort. He'd already kissed her, so that line had been left in the dust a long time ago. "Since you are past the first and second blooms of youth, may I ask why you aren't attached? Perhaps you were a war bride and now a widow?" Of course, mentioning her supposed age and her lack of martial status wasn't well done of him, but he couldn't recall the words.

"Oh. How rude of you to drive home the point that I am unmarried." Some of the color faded from her face. "I *was* engaged once, so it wasn't as if I was unwanted. There is a difference, you know."

"Of course there is." Why did she want to impress that point on him? How interesting. "What happened? Did he die?"

"No, but there were times when I wished he would have."

Lewis could do nothing but gawk at her. "What?" Was he inadvertently harboring a criminal?

She stood, apparently restless, and with her arms wrapped around herself, she began to pace in front of the sofa. "I was engaged at a young age—nineteen. At the time, my father was a celebrated ship captain; everyone in society adored him and he was sought after to make up numbers at dinner parties and routs."

"I believe we have done business with your father in some capacity over the recent months, but Alexander handles the books, so I may be speaking out of turn." None of that mattered and it certainly didn't pertain to the current conversation.

A sigh escaped her. "Because of that, he made many connections, and one of them was a viscount who had a son a few years older than me."

"Ah, and because he is a caring father, he wanted you to make a good connection within the *ton*, so he endorsed the match." It was a story told time out of hand. "What happened?"

"At first, everything went well. He was attentive and romantic and everything I thought a fiancé should be." She paused in her pacing to stare out the rear window. "A few months into the engagement, things changed—he changed."

"In what way?" But his chest tightened, for he both didn't want to know and was dying to discover the truth at the same time.

"He had a temper, and when he lost at the gaming tables or when misfortune of any kind came his way, he would take out those frustrations on me, which resulted in multiple bruises, and once, he nearly broke my arm. Of course, he always apologized after the incidents happened, told me they would never happen again. At first I believed him… until it continued."

"The bounder!" Before he could understand his reaction, Lewis sprang up from the sofa. "Give me his name, and I will go clean his clock."

When she turned about to face him, her tiny smile had his chest tightening for a completely different reason. "While that is a lovely thing to say, I refuse to voice his name aloud. That time in my life is over." Her chin trembled as she met his gaze. "Finally, I told my father about the beatings. He immediately paid a call to the man, threatened many things, and from what he told me, ran him out of Town, for I haven't seen my fiancé since."

Once more, Lewis gawked at her. "Was the engagement broken?"

"I would imagine. My father was the last person to have words with him. Due to the delicate nature of the circumstances surrounding the abrupt end to the engagement, Papa as well as the viscount thought it best to say my former fiancé had important and sensitive pressing business in America, and instead of wishing to continue the engagement indefinitely, all parties agreed to end it."

"Ah, and thereby saving your reputation."

She nodded. "Among other reasons."

"Meaning?" Why were there still so many secrets lurking in her eyes?

"It is neither here nor there."

"How long were you with your fiancé?"

"Not more than a year."

"And you never wished to try again?"

A blush stained her pale cheeks. "Perhaps here and there, but after such a thing happens to a woman, trust that is lost is all too difficult to rebuild."

Lewis nodded. "Understandable."

She heaved a sigh. "When I began having problems with men at the docks, my patience with men snapped." Resolve reflected in her eyes. "That is why I wished to learn how to box. I need a way to defend myself. My father says I should stay at home, that he'll bring the ledgers and paperwork to me, but if I do that, I allow the bullies to win and honestly, I don't wish to have my wings clipped, so to speak." Then a plea entered those blue pools. "Please don't cancel our lessons, Mr. Stapleton. I couldn't bear it, and that would feel all too much like defeat."

Well, damn. How could he send her away now?

"All right. Calm yourself, please." He shoved a hand through his hair. There was a responsibility to the salon, but he also had one toward her. "We can continue the lessons at your home."

"I would rather we didn't, for there are servants underfoot and my brother has his tutors throughout the week."

"Very well. Then your father's shipping office?"

"That would work. Rarely is he there on Tuesdays and Thursdays. Those are the days when he meets with investors and clients, and when he inspects cargo coming off ships." Her eyes were luminous with tears. "Thank you, Mr. Stapleton."

I am the biggest nodcock in the world, all for a pair of jewel-like eyes. But he nodded like a dunce. "Please call me Lewis."

"All right… Lewis. I am Cecilia." Then she smiled, and he thought his world might upend if he didn't grab hold of something. Before, the shortened version of her name had slipped out in the moment, but now he officially could use her given name. It was quite the boon. "Shall we resume next week?"

"And miss days? Hardly." With a queer feeling in the pit of his stomach, he briefly pressed his lips together. "Come here to the salon on Sunday. We don't open on that day, but I'll meet you here. Wear your usual boy's attire, and I will keep the alley door unlocked so you can easily slip in before anyone sees you. We will do more sparring at that time."

"I appreciate that so much. You have no idea." Then she collected her cap and set it back over her blonde tresses. "Have a lovely afternoon, Lewis."

The way she said his name, as if her lips caressed the word before releasing it into the air, was like poetry. Such thoughts pushed him further toward madness, surely. "You as well, Cecilia." Then he cleared his throat, for something kept poking at him. "Uh, why did you kiss me?"

At the door, she shrugged. "Oddly, I felt safe with you, as if I were protected. Somehow, I knew you wouldn't hurt me where others have." It was said in such a matter-of-fact tone that he couldn't help but believe it as truth. "That being said, why did you return the kiss?"

Heat went up the back of his neck. *Was* there an easy answer? "I wanted to because there is something about you that makes me feel… different. I can't explain it." That would have to suffice.

"Fair enough." Then, with a nod, she opened the door to his office and was gone with his next breath.

How the devil was he to explain this to his brothers?

Chapter Six

June 22, 1817
Stapleton Boxing Salon
Mayfair, London

WHEN CECILIA PUSHED open the door to the boxing salon, her gaze went immediately to the man at the wooden frame where the punching bags hung. Oh, dear heavens, it was the earl, and he'd stripped to his breeches, for he was currently pummeling one of the sand-filled bags. From all accounts, it seemed he was working through some hidden emotions, for his face was like a thundercloud.

"Lewis?"

Slowly, she approached but kept her gaze on that bared torso as if she'd never seen a half-clothed man. Perhaps she hadn't, for he was unlike anyone she'd laid eyes on before. A mat of light brown hair covered the upper portion of his chest in an abstract butterfly pattern. His muscles played beneath his skin with every punch he drilled into the sandbag, and that was when she became aware of how powerful his arms and chest truly were. When he glanced at her from around the sandbag, there was a thin sheen of sweat that glistened over his skin.

"Cecilia. I didn't hear you come in." Welcome lit his hazel eyes, like twin gorgeous works of art in the anemic sunlight that streamed through the front windows. "I was, ah, getting in a workout before our lesson officially starts."

"By all means, don't let me interrupt you," she said in a voice that was quite a bit more breathless than she'd intended. The ridges of his abdomen caught and held her attention, and suddenly she knew a powerful urge to lick syllabub or even champagne from his skin.

Pull yourself together, Ceci. He is not for you, and you don't need a man in your life in such fashion. Have you learned nothing?

"I haven't had the time to focus on my own fitness since the salon opened." He took up a towel of woven linen, then wiped at the sweat on his brow and face. "Yet it's critical a boxer remain in top form."

"So I would imagine." There were many questions about him she wanted to ask, but now didn't seem the time. "It probably helps also to work out aggressions or clear your thoughts."

"A bit. I still carry heavy responsibility even after punching the hell out of the bags."

She cocked an eyebrow at his use of vulgarity, but it wasn't that offensive. She'd heard worse while working at the docks. "Are we still having our lesson today?"

"We are." When he gestured toward a table in the corner where padded mittens rested, he said, "Collect a pair of mittens. I'll start you on the bags today."

"All right." After removing her cap and her tweed jacket, she dumped the garments onto the floor near the wall behind the punching bags. "You still wish for my hands to be protected? If I'm accosted on the street, I will not have mittens."

"While this is true, I do not want your knuckles bloody and busted, for while a man might go about society with such and no one will say much, if a woman does the same, talk will jump from the dinner table to all over Town in three seconds." As he wiped his chest with the towel, she followed the movement with her gaze. "You don't need to find yourself a victim of the silver-tongued gossips."

Warmth filled her chest, but she chose not to comment as she picked out a pair of mittens she liked. "I appreciate that. However-er, I rarely go out into society these days." Truly, her life had grown quite dull, and she hadn't been aware of that until she'd started coming to the boxing salon.

"I'm sorry to hear that." The earl tossed the towel on the floor near her discarded garments.

"Why?" She frowned at him as she drifted back into his orbit, and he helped her to don the mittens.

"You are an attractive woman whose father is an upstanding member of the *ton*, and a gentleman from all I understand," he said with a shrug, then pulled the laces of one of the gloves tight. "Does your past history make you frightened of doing brave things?"

"Some." As he did up the laces on the second glove, Cecilia had difficulties concentrating on the conversation with him half-clothed and so close. The scent of his shaving soap and cologne mingled with the earthier scent of man in her nose, and her pulse increased. Did it make her a fool that she enjoyed and appreciated this man's form even while she'd made incredibly stupid choices in her past? To be fair, she'd been led down the garden path by her former fiancé, but shouldn't she have more discernment? Yanking herself out of her thoughts, she sighed. "I have apparent-ly no intuition when it comes to men, and quite frankly, I don't wish to try again only to find myself disappointed or broken again."

The admission might make her more vulnerable or an object of pity to him, but she couldn't help but be authentic. Life was too short for anything else.

A muscle in his cheek ticced as he nodded. "Consider this, though. Many of us are broken; that doesn't necessarily mean we are useless." He moved behind her and nudged her over to one of the bags. "This one is filled with straw. I've put you onto this one before, but go ahead and throw a few punches until you're familiar with your stance and form, then we'll graduate you to the other one."

How was she expected to concentrate on that task when the heat of him seeped into her body? Cecilia did as instructed, and there was a familiarity there with the mittens from when she used them during her last lesson. "This is different than hitting your hands." When she drilled a mittened fist into the straw bag, it didn't have the same satisfying purchase as hitting his hands had.

"While I understand, in this way you can correct your approach as well get a feel for the differences in things you might encounter during an attack. Men's bodies are not the same."

Well, that was an understatement, for it was night and day between Lewis and Mr. Derrickson. She nodded, and continued to hit the straw-filled bag with her right hand.

"Use both, Lia. Your attacker certainly will."

Punch.

"But I'm not as strong with my left."

"That won't matter when either your life is in jeopardy, or an attacker is trying to rape you." His expression was sober and his eyes like hard pieces of green sea glass when she met his gaze. "You'll want every shred of skill and fight with you if that happens."

"Thank you for the reminder." Emboldened and slightly worried, Cecilia made a point to utilize her left hand more.

Punch.

"Remember, your knuckles guide the punch." His voice was at her ear as the earl stepped close. He took hold of her left hand, corrected her stance. "Even with mittens, don't forget the basics. Once you master those, you will be unstoppable." The heat of his breath skated along her nape. "I can't wait for that day."

"Does that mean our lessons will go on indefinitely?"

Punch, punch.

"Not indefinitely, but certainly for the conceivable future."

Another few punches came from her, and though she was weaker with her left, with some practice, her confidence would grow. Sweat rolled down her back, pasting her linen shirt to her skin, and the muscles in her arms began to ache, but she enjoyed the exercise. There was a certain amount of freedom there knowing she was learning how to defend herself.

"Lewis?" She half turned toward him, found him watching her with an intensity that sent heightened awareness sailing over her skin.

"Hmm?" When his gaze dropped to her mouth, a shiver of need went down her spine.

"Will you and I spar again today?"

"I wager we will, in a few ways." He put a hand to her elbow. "Do you enjoy sparring?"

"Very much. I look forward to learning even more about the sport. It's fascinating." She gazed up at him, for she was at least a handful of inches shorter than he. "Also, you are a lovely teacher."

In more ways than one.

"Are you always so honest?"

"Why would I lie? There is no value in it." She shrugged. "Over the years, I've learned to take joy in the little moments where I can, because life has the potential to turn horrid all too soon."

For long moments, he held her gaze, and his eyes shifted to that green hue again. "Come with me."

"Where?"

"My office."

"Why?" She couldn't help but frown as she struggled to keep pace with him as he guided her into the familiar space.

"Because I have apparently lost my damned mind." As soon as they both had come into the room, Lewis caught her into his arms and brought his lips crashing down on hers.

Merciful heavens, this is becoming quite the habit!

For a fleeting second, Cecilia froze, met his gaze with surprise and shivering need coursing through her veins, but then she uttered a sigh mixed with a moan, looped her arms about his shoulders regardless of the padded mittens on her hands, and applied herself to kissing him back.

It was much as if a match had been dropped onto a pile of tinder.

In next to no time, something akin to a fire consumed her. What was it about this man in this time of her life that had her acting the wanton merely to experience another kiss? There were no answers, and at the back of her mind, she wondered if this was how she should have felt when she first became engaged years ago.

Or even more darkly, would the earl become something she hadn't seen yet?

All thoughts flew out of her head when Lewis walked her backward until the window prevented further movement. Then he slipped his hands beneath her thighs and hefted her upward, pressing her back against the glass and trapping her between that and his body.

Dear God, if anyone came into the salon, what they were doing would be fully on display. And suddenly, it didn't matter. For too long, she hadn't given herself permission to enjoy life, and this was a moment of joy that would be over far too quickly. He tasted of coffee and sin and scandal; it was a heady combination that she chased with every frantic meeting of their mouths.

When he ran the tip of his tongue along the seam of her lips, she opened for him. The second his tongue touched hers and the glide of satin and silk made the connection with her brain, Cecilia was in danger of being lost. Over and over again, he fenced with her, explored her mouth, tangled with her tongue, and it was all she could do to keep up with those heated kisses.

In order to find better purchase, she slipped her legs about his waist and locked her ankles at the small of his back. She wasn't quite so innocent that she didn't notice the bulge of his erection rubbing against the center of her. The friction at the rapidly swelling nubbin sent flutters of need careening down her spine to lodge between her thighs.

When a tiny mewl escaped her, quickly followed by a barely audible moan, he growled in response. And it simply wasn't enough. Wanting more, craving it even, Cecilia nibbled and nipped at his bottom lip, then left his mouth entirely to press featherweighted kisses beneath his jaw. The smell of him, the taste of him, the heat of his bare chest all worked at her undoing.

Why didn't I remove the mittens so at least I could touch him!

There were no answers, not in that moment where she fell through heat and passion and plain lust. In this moment, she felt wanted when she hadn't been for such a long time, and had kept herself removed from even being close to a man.

"Bloody hell, Lia, what are you doing to me?" Renewing his grip on her thighs, Lewis turned her about, and still kissing her, he moved them to his desk. When he planted her arse upon it, a pile of invoices fluttered to the hardwood floor.

They both ignored the mess.

"I don't know, but I can't understand why this keeps happening between us," she whispered and felt as if she were flying through fog.

"We should probably have more decorum or willpower." His voice was a graveled whisper while he encouraged her backward over the desktop. As he settled himself between her splayed thighs, he dragged his lips down the side of her throat. When undoing the strings that held her borrowed shirt closed, he uttered a huff of apparent frustration, for then he grunted and yanked the shirttails from her breeches.

"You're right. This isn't proper at all." Did it matter? They were both past the age of majority, and she had been on the shelf for a long while already. Nearly gone, Cecilia managed to wrench a padded mitten from her right hand, and once she did, her fingers went to his nape, pulling him closer. She put her lips to the hollow of his throat, then drew her fingertips down his naked chest, reveling at the tactile feel of him as his breath steamed her cheek.

"It is not." Yet that didn't deter him, for he slipped his hands beneath her shirt to cup her breasts.

When he kneaded them, the sensations tugged a surprised

moan from her throat. She grinned against his mouth, but as he brushed the pads of his thumbs over her hardening nipples, she moaned as if she had no shame. "Lewis…" Familiar tingles zipped up and down her spine, for she remembered this from her engagement, but it was so different with the earl. As her back arched the longer he played, he shoved up the shirt so he could take one of the buds into his mouth. "Oh!" How was it possible to feel like flying with him, when this act had been fear-laden with her fiancé? While he continued to torment the nipple with his lips and teeth, he teased the other with his thumb. "This is…" Her words dissolved beneath another moan of pleasure. "Do *that* again."

"So responsive." A chuckle escaped as he again flicked his tongue over that tip.

Was that a good thing or a bad thing? Fires erupted in her blood. Oh, how she wanted to give herself over into this man's care, but something held her back, a tiny niggle of fear that played her spine, yet he made her feel so wonderful it was confusing. Did it mean he was merely like all the rest of the men she'd come into contact with, and he only wanted access to her body? She knew nothing about him beyond what pertained to the boxing salon. That would prove problematic. "Lewis, I have…" The questions vanished beneath another wave of pleasure. When he took her other nipple into his mouth, her arm with the padded mitten still attached flailed outward. A ledger book tumbled to the floor with a loud thud.

The noise must have jarred the earl from his task, for he pulled slightly backward and peered down at her with darkened eyes. "Good thing we're alone, hmm?"

Except the sound of an exhalation of breath at the door echoed loudly in the sudden hush of the room. "What the devil is going on in here?"

And that wasn't a product of her imagination.

"Alexander, what the hell are you doing here? It's Sunday." The low rumble of the earl's voice reverberated in her chest, and as he turned about to face the man she vaguely remembered as his brother, he shielded her from the newcomer's gaze while she scrambled to tug the padded mitten off her left hand.

Oh, no! As Cecilia struggled into a seated position on the desk and tried to set her borrowed clothing to rights, she unashamedly listened to their conversation.

The other man, perhaps a couple of years younger than Lewis, bounced his gaze between them as amusement lined his face. "I thought to come here and tackle the books and invoices in the quiet where I wouldn't be interrupted, but obviously the desk is being used for other… endeavors just now."

Embarrassed heat fired in her cheeks. She slithered off the desk. "I should go."

The odd mix of pleading and panic in Lewis' eyes as he darted a glance at her stayed her flight. "Please stay. At least for a bit." A muscle in his cheek ticced. "I apologize for taking advantage of you."

Though she nodded, the other man—Alexander—spoke before she could. "My brother is correct, Miss…?"

"Dawson," she said in a quiet voice.

"Miss Dawson. Please stay." His grin was wide but genuine as he rested his gaze, so like his brother's, on her. "Even more so since you have seemed to garner the interest of my brother. That instantly makes you interesting." He stepped around Lewis and extended a hand to her. "Hullo. I am Viscount Wexley, but you may call me Alexander. I have a feeling this won't be the last time I see you."

If possible, the heat in her cheeks intensified. "Lovely to meet you." Barely had she slipped her hand into the viscount's when Lewis uttered a sound suspiciously like a growl and broke their contact.

"Enough. Alex, you should go." As he crossed his arms at his chest, he scowled.

Which seemed to amuse his brother even further. "Not likely." He focused his attention on the earl. "Miss Dawson is a lovely woman. You should go out into society with her, Lewis."

He scowled even more fiercely. "She is a student. We are not in a courtship."

"One could argue that point since you are half naked and she was sprawled over your desk in her own form of undress." But there was no censure in the viscount's voice. "Obviously, you have a connection with the lady, so you should court her."

"Do shut up," was all Lewis said, while Cecilia looked on in some interest.

"I won't." Alexander shook his head as his grin grew wider. "What's wrong with Miss Dawson? I imagine when she'd not dressed as a boy, she is quite pretty." He tossed a glance her way, and her cheeks heated again. "Are you by chance related to a Captain Dawson?"

Though it was odd, this standing between two brothers on the heels of a scandalous embrace, she was thrilled that someone knew her father. "He is my father. Are you a contemporary of his?"

"No, but I know of him, and I see his name on the ledger books." He gave her a wink, much to the annoyance of the earl. "We purchase equipment, and the fabric for the sand and straw bags, through his shipping outfit."

"Oh!" She gasped. Were the brothers the new client her father had spoken of a month or so ago? "How interesting."

"Indeed." The viscount nodded. "Also, I could swear he was friends with my father."

"I believe that too. Papa said as much regarding the earl a couple of days ago to me when I mentioned I was taking lessons here." She stooped to collect the scattered invoices as well as the ledger book that had fallen from the desk. "If you should run into problems with the accounting, I'd be willing to assist you. It's what I do for my father's office; numbers have always come easy to me."

"Ah, I might just ask you to do that, for numbers vex me." Alexander rushed to assist her in putting everything onto the desktop. "Has my reprobate brother told you that he'll be fighting in a public bout tomorrow?"

"What?" With another gasp, she glanced at the earl. "You fight outside of this salon?"

"I do upon occasion. For coin." He unbent enough to search out a shirt in one of the drawers of his desk. "When my shoulder and knee allow."

What did that mean? "Have you sustained injuries from the sport, then?"

"Some, but they haven't killed me yet." Quickly, he smoothed the fine lawn garment over his head and down his torso as he shoved his arms into the sleeves.

She frowned when he covered that lovely expanse of naked chest. "I see."

Alexander chuckled. "How much has she ascertained about boxing and you?"

"I don't know." A dark flush rose up the earl's neck. "Enough. I suppose."

"Ha!" A snort issued from Cecilia. "Not *nearly* enough, about him or boxing." When she transferred her attention to the viscount, she shrugged. "He doesn't talk about himself."

"That sounds like Lewis." The cheeky grin didn't fade from his face. "So I'll give you a quick history. Because our father squandered the family fortune, we're not far from dun territory so we need to make income. Lewis is trying to win prize purses that will help with that. Duncan and I are also taking slots in bouts." As he talked, he moved closer to her. "If you want to know the truth of the matter, I'm the better boxer, but not nearly as good as Duncan. I'm also much more charming."

"That's quite enough, Alex," the earl warned, but his brother paid him no heed.

"Miss Dawson, if Lewis fails to interest you, I'd be more than happy to escort you about Town. Perhaps take you driving on Rotten Row, do all the usual summertime things *ton* ladies enjoy." He winked again. "I wouldn't mind having such a woman on my arm."

"Oh!" What had she done in her life to have two men from the same family showing an interest in her?

"Over my dead body," Lewis said in a voice that echoed with sounds of a growl. It was quite possessive, but it was more protective as he moved toward her.

She frowned at him. Outside of the two kisses she had shared with the earl, he hadn't made any such offers to interact with her beyond the bounds of the salon, not that she'd encouraged him, but it was lovely to think that a handsome man might wish to. "It's truly a wonderful offer, Lord Wexley, and I wouldn't mind—"

"No." Lewis shook his head. Briefly, he touched a hand to the small of her back before breaking the connection when Alexander eyed him with speculation. "Leave her alone, Alex. She is *not* for you. Or even Duncan for that matter."

"Oh?" One of the other man's eyebrows rose in challenge. "Why not? *You* apparently don't know how to treat a woman."

Another flush rose up Lewis' neck. "Miss Dawson deserves much more than to be squired about for a few weeks, bedded, then abandoned as is your usual way of things. She is *not* destined to be someone's mistress or plaything."

"Ah, so then what I just saw you doing with her must have been something different?"

The sarcasm was apparently lost on the earl, for both she and the viscount stared at him.

Finally, Alexander chuckled. "That's rather how Duncan lives *his* life. I'd be different, but I can see how you already have laid down a claim on Miss Dawson even if you don't know that yet." Dismissing him, the viscount turned the full of his attention on her. "Would you enjoy attending the bout with me as my guest? It will be early enough that we can all return to Town before dinner. You can come to the salon disguised. I'll escort you there so you can watch Lewis fight, and find out what bare-knuckle boxing is truly about."

That sounded all too interesting, and if it would afford her another chance to see the earl shirtless, why shouldn't she?

Besides, it might help her understand him better, and there was no harm in it since she would be in a disguise. Of course, being in that company would see her reputation ruined if something were to happen… "I would enjoy that. Thank you."

"The bout is tomorrow around midday. They are usually on the weekends, but it depends on who is organizing the bouts. In the outskirts of Surrey. Meet me here around nine o'clock in the morning."

"I will." She nodded.

Lewis blew out a breath as he captured his brother in his annoyed gaze. "You realize I am traveling with you and Duncan, don't you?"

"I do, but since you are acting like a Barbarian, I thought I'd play the gentleman in front of Miss Dawson so she can easily see the contrast between us."

While she bit her bottom lip to keep from laughing, the earl glowered. "Do shut up, Alex. I won't ask you again." For long moments, the brothers stared each other down.

"And after the bout?" the viscount asked, clearly not backing down, which was providential because she was interested in the outcome as well.

"Fine." Lewis blew out a breath of apparent frustration or even resignation. "I will take Miss Dawson out into society, perhaps a trip to the British Museum. I owe her at least that."

"Good." With a wide grin, Alex winked at her. "It seems I have much to look forward to in the upcoming days." Then he made a shooing motion with his hands. "Now, the two of you need to get out of this office. I have accounting work to take care of."

Cecilia nodded. "And our lesson isn't over." After retrieving her discarded padded mittens, she left the office with a queer little spring to her step, for it felt rather as if she were teetering on the edge of something far larger than boxing lessons.

But what? Nothing much had changed, except the desire she had for the earl continued to grow. That was a problem for another day.

Chapter Seven

June 23, 1817
Worchester, Surrey

LEWIS FROWNED AS he surveyed the large clearing of grass where the bout would take place. Since bare-knuckle boxing, especially for profit, was illegal within the bounds of London proper, most bouts took place in surrounding areas. The sites were often farm fields, or clearings—even better—for sometimes thousands of spectators would assemble. Since it had only taken a couple of hours to travel from London to the area where the bout was being held, there had been little to no fatigue from sitting in the coach, and they'd taken the closed one in the event that it rained during their comings or goings. The only thing that had made the trip palatable was the fact Cecilia had been among their numbers. Throughout the trip, conversation was lively, and he'd found himself chuckling more than once, and much of that was due to her. Between jokes and scandalous stories his brothers regaled her with, his brothers kept up a steady stream of conversation with her in which he'd discovered she adored the roasted sugared nuts found at Covent Gardens in the evening, that she felt responsible for guiding her brother through life in lieu of their dead mother, and that she envied her father in that he'd travelled on a ship on the seas.

And he was even more fascinated with her than he'd been

before.

Now, as Duncan came abreast of him, Lewis shook himself from his thoughts, for they would do him no good right before the bout.

"Looks to be a decent crowd," he said to his brother as a couple of men—no doubt sponsors of the event—were walking a space of the clearing and driving posts into the ground. It would be where they wrapped ropes about them to cordon off the area and designate it as a ring of sorts.

"Indeed," Duncan said with a nod as he glanced about. "Perhaps a few hundred. Not bad, and if the wagering is fierce, all the better." He frowned at Lewis. "How do you feel?"

"Well enough." He refused to let on to the fact that he currently suffered from nerves and apprehension. What if his shoulder or knee decided to give out during this bout? And he certainly didn't wish to make a fool of himself with Cecilia watching. "It is nothing I can't muddle through. Do you know who my opponent will be today?"

His brother shrugged. "I haven't been told. The boxer slated for the event backed out at the last moment due to having his clock cleaned at a tavern two nights prior, but I'll talk with the organizer and find out who the replacement is as well as start working the crowd."

"Thank you." Once Duncan left him, he sought out Alexander, who'd promised to keep Cecilia within his sight, at least until the bout began, for Alex was his knee man. When he caught his eye, Lewis moved toward them both. "Lia, if you find all of this too overwhelming, no one would fault you for wishing to remain in the coach."

She shook her head. "I am made of sterner stuff, Your Lordship. A bit of blood or violence won't shock me, especially after what I have already survived," she added in a low voice. "Besides, I'm curious. Once I watch a boxing match, I will perhaps understand better how to move my own body."

"Fair enough." He nodded, for he couldn't let his concern for her safety circumvent his concentration on the upcoming bout. "It should begin soon, so stay close and don't do anything to call attention to who you are beneath the disguise." Though he could immediately identify her as a woman, he hoped no one else looked too closely. Bringing home the prize purse was far too important than acting the nodcock about a woman.

With a glance at Alexander, who shrugged, Cecilia moved toward Lewis and then laid a hand briefly on his arm. Reaction shot up that limb to the elbow. "Be careful. Your brother has told me of your injuries and that any sort of hard hit to either of those areas could bring you down." The concern in the blue pools of her eyes arrested him. "I am looking forward to seeing what you're made of. I know you'll prove impressive."

For whatever reason, those words had his confidence soaring. "Thank you. I'll do my level best." Then, with a nod, he moved off to join Duncan where he talked with an official. It wouldn't be long now.

THE ENERGY FROM the gathered crowd fed into Lewis' nerves, and that made him anxious to get on with the fight. Would Cecilia find his form pleasing, his footwork impressive, his punches thrilling?

Why the devil do I care?

He damn well knew why, but he'd be dead before he admitted he was beginning to fall beneath the woman's spell, especially when all she'd been was her authentic self who only wished to learn how to fight so she could take back her life. But he'd promised his brother that he would escort her out into society.

To what purpose?

That remained to be seen.

"Woolgathering will see you trounced out there," Alexander chided, and the sound of his voice brought Lewis back to the present. "You should be thinking about the fight." A hint of censure rang in his tone. "From what I've been given to understand, Oliver Ulstead won't go down easily."

"Agreed."

"Gossip says he's a viscount's son."

"Well, we all have to belong to someone, don't we?" Lewis shook his head to clear his thoughts. Cecilia had no place in his mind when there were other more important things in his immediate future, like winning this prize purse. He stripped to the waist and handed his clothes to his brother, who would serve as his knee man during the bout. Basically, that meant Alex would offer him his knee like a footstool to provide a modicum of rest between rounds. "I'm focused."

"Glad to hear it." Alexander looked at him with narrowed eyes. "How many times have you been with Miss Dawson as you were yesterday?" he asked in a whisper, for Cecilia waited near one of the corner posts, looking for all the world like a woman in boy's clothing.

God, please keep her safe.

"That time only," he said a little too quickly. "Plus, one other kiss," he admitted without glancing her way. Those bloody kisses had changed everything, yet he hadn't given her anything in return. What sort of a man refused to talk about himself when she'd willingly shared with him so much about her life and past?

"Why do I not believe you?" Alex questioned with speculation in his eyes. "And why the devil choose her? You're an earl for Christ's sake. You could have your pick of any woman in the *beau monde.*"

Why indeed. "She's different." With Lia, there were no games, no flirting. A man knew where he stood with her, and she wasn't afraid to put him in his place. Of course, she'd never said she wished for a courtship... "I suppose it's because she needs someone."

Suddenly, he wanted to be her champion, to show her that not all men were scoundrels and bounders. And, dash it all, he wished to become her teacher in other things beyond the sparring field.

If she'd let him regardless of what his brothers or mother would think.

Then a shrill whistle blast pierced the air and scattered his wayward thoughts.

"Damn. He hadn't been aware his opponent or the judge had entered the ring.

A short, stout man stood in the middle of the boxing square and held up a hand. "We're about to begin." When the noise from the crowd died down somewhat, he continued, "Today's match is between crowd favorite Lewis Stapleton, or you may know him as the Earl of Lethbridge." A roar erupted from the men assembled as spectators. "And his rival, the man who's trounced more than his fair share of boxers, Mr. Oliver Ulstead." Another cheer rose from the crowd.

When Lewis happened to glance over his shoulder at Cecilia, he frowned for all the blood had drained from her face and her gaze was fixed upon the man at the opposite side of the boxing ring, standing in his own corner.

"Lia, is something amiss?"

"Yes." She nodded as she focused on his face. "That man was my fiancé. I thought... I assumed he'd gone away from England..."

The man who had beaten her on a regular basis. The viscount's son. *Well, damn.*

There was no time to ponder what this meant, but he wanted to clean the man's clock. "I..."

"Put your head in the game, man," Alexander hissed in a whisper as he shoved at Lewis' shoulder.

"Right." He briefly touched Cecilia's hand before scanning the crowd of men who shouted their approval and support. "I'll get you the justice you should have had from him years ago," he promised her in a low voice.

A wash of tears filled her eyes, but she nodded as Duncan came over to stand at her side. "I'll stay close to Lord Frampton."

Clearly, Duncan had told her what his title was, since it had been his right at birth to make one for himself as an earl's son.

"He'll look after you, but I have to go." After exchanging looks with Alex, Lewis moved toward the judge in the center of the roped off ring.

Mr. Ulstead also loped toward the judge—a barrel-chested man with full eyebrows and a tall, proud bearing. His mop of black hair was tousled and curled slightly, but the man resembled a bear and would no doubt wield the same power of that animal.

"This fight will go quickly, Lethbridge," Ulstead growled. He flashed a grin of premature victory. "Gossip holds that you're aging and weak."

"We'll see about that." Lewis flexed his hands, then lifted his arms above his head and performed a few stretches. As he stared into the face of the man who'd love nothing more than to beat him into the sweet-smelling meadow grass, he knew a profound urge to bust up his opponent's handsome face for what he'd done to Lia.

And for all the ills she probably hadn't told him about. That needed to change. Regardless of whether he wanted to pursue a courtship with her, he owed her his full attention and a sharing of the man he truly was behind the guise of the earl or the boxing instructor. Renewed energy flowed through Lewis' veins, and he assumed his first position, fists at the ready, body taut and balanced. "May the best man win, Ulstead."

A whistle blast split the air. The judge shouted, "Remember, rounds will continue until one man is put on the ground and unable to stand after three seconds. Go!"

Lewis and his opponent circled each other, prowled through the meadow grass of the eight-foot roped off area. Two judges waited in opposite corners. How best to bring the brute down? It was a difficult order, but he'd find a way. Anticipation rode his spine, prompting him into movement. He threw the first punch. It connected solidly with Ulstead's cheek without much effect.

"Is that the best you've got, Lethbridge?" The other man

grinned as he struck out a powerful fist.

Lewis danced away, much to the crowd's roar of approval. "I'm just getting started." He swung a fist, but the bigger man easily dodged the punch.

"Time to go down." Ulstead struck with a fast uppercut to Lewis' chin that jarred his teeth together.

Pain exploded through his face, but he held his ground and returned the volley. Then they were into the thick of the first round as blows rained and fists pummeled, landing on solid flesh in rhythmic intervals. One of his punches had Ulstead staggering backward, but the man didn't fall. Neither did Lewis when retaliation occurred.

Minutes ticked by that seemed like hours. His left shoulder protested, and his breath grew labored before the round was finally called.

Grateful for the brief reprieve, Lewis trudged to his corner, as did Ulstead. "I might have underestimated Ulstead's tenacity." Of course, he had the stamina of an abuser. He perched upon Alexander's knee while Cecilia watched from outside the ring with wide eyes.

"Stop whining." Duncan handed Lewis a ladle full of cool water from an oaken bucket. "You're trailing him; you need to move your feet faster."

"Indeed." Lewis wiped sweat from his brow with a rag. After taking a deep sip from the ladle, he handed it back to his brother.

"It's nothing you haven't faced before." Alexander rubbed down the muscles in Lewis' shoulders. His left one ached liked the devil. "Keep going and wear him down. Your footwork never fails."

"I trust my skill." Yet if he gave himself permission, he'd take down the other man and pummel him into the dirt for what he did to Cecilia.

Another whistle blast announced the start of round two, and Lewis returned to the middle of the ring to face off with his opponent once more.

"I've had about enough of you, Lethbridge," Ulstead growled out. "Step aside and let us younger boxers have our reign."

"I'd rather die," he tossed back.

"I can arrange that."

"Like hell." Movement and a flash of bright color at one side of the ring caught his eye. Daring to peek, Lewis gasped even as his pulse kicked up. Cecilia, shrouded in her black cloak and male clothing, had moved along the ropes for a better view, concern etched on her face. How could anyone not see that she was a woman?

A hard uppercut to his jaw had him staggering back several steps. The crowd roared and as one entity surged forward. Quite fickle in their support, it seemed, but then, people liked to see blood. Pain exploded through his head, but he kept his feet. This was why having a woman in his life was an exceedingly bad idea. Too much distraction, especially her. Putting Lia firmly from his mind, Lewis lunged toward his opponent with a grunt. He landed quick jabs to Ulstead's gut and cheek.

The man reeled and retreated before gathering himself and charging at Lewis to exchange blows.

Again and again, he drilled his fists into the bigger man's body, but the boxer wouldn't fall.

Ulstead got off a few good punches of his own, and the determination Lewis had always been known for kept him on his feet, though winded and hurting.

"I'm going to put you down for what you did to Cecilia," Lewis taunted, even though he wanted to cry out from the pain in his shoulder.

Surprise flickered in the other man's eyes. "How the hell do you know her?"

"You don't deserve to know that." And he delivered a swift right hook to the other man's cheek that sent the other man spinning about. Though he staggered, he didn't fall.

Then the round was once again called without a clear victor.

Lewis stumbled back to his corner, dropping heavily onto

Alexander's bent knee, panting. He rubbed his left shoulder with his right hand. "I went too far," he admitted in a whisper.

"What the devil ails you?" Alexander hissed, as Duncan plied him with water. "You're all over the place out there."

"I know, and I goaded him verbally to catch him off guard."

"Well, stop that and put him down."

"I'm trying, but he's more powerful." Lewis stood, glancing at Cecilia, who stood behind his corner. When their gazes connected, she offered a tremulous smile. Heated sensation went through him, followed by a blossom of hope that lifted his flagging spirits, but when her notice went back to his opponent and fear jumped into her eyes, he vowed to make certain Ulstead knew he wasn't welcome in London.

"Damn it, Lewis, get your head out of your arse," Alexander hissed, and gave him a push, which refocused his wandering thoughts.

"Right."

The judge blew his whistle again. The next round was imminent.

"It's dangerous to have your concentration split." Alexander slapped his shoulder. The sting of pain brought Lewis back to the task at hand. "Go." He shoved him, and it propelled him to the center of the ring for round three.

Ulstead came out swinging, literally. Lewis was caught up in a whirlwind of blows that left him reeling. When one of the bigger man's fists drilled into his left shoulder, pain swamped him, had him doubled up with pain. Another blow gave him a bloody nose and the sickening crunch of cartilage. There was no hint of gentlemanly fighting here. The bout had become rough and tumble street fighting.

And he welcomed it.

Lewis took a deep breath and retaliated using a quick double uppercut, one with each fist despite the pain in his shoulder, and then followed those with a blow to the man's temple.

But Ulstead didn't go down.

From seemingly a long distance, Cecilia's cry of encouragement sank into his brain, discerned somehow over the roar and cheers from the crowd. His heart squeezed to know she continued to support him even when he wasn't making his best showing. Alexander yelled for him to keep moving.

Footwork as well as strategic punches would win the day; they always did. He could do this. Above all, he couldn't let the distraction of Cecilia take him out. Straightening his spine, he blew out a breath and once more faced his opponent. Stupidly, he wanted to appear a hero in Cecilia's eyes to elevate his status, make her think he was more than what he was.

Perhaps to restore his faith in his own existence. *I have to be more than merely an earl with a nearly empty title.*

"Give up already, Lethbridge. I'm twice the boxer you are." Ulstead snarled and snapped his teeth as he circled. "And you haven't aged well."

"Sorry to disappoint you." Every movement he made brought spikes of pain to different places in his body, but he entered the fray once more.

"Stubborn arse." Ulstead came on like the brute he was. He had strength on his side. "Your time as London's darling is at an end. You aren't the fighter your father was."

"I never tried to be." The words dented his confidence. Lewis defended the best he could, but it was as if he were fighting a hurricane and being battered from all sides. Though he rallied a few times, punch after punch was exchanged, and Ulstead barely slowed his assault.

As the match wore on, round followed round, and Lewis endurance wavered. His stamina waned. Blood dripped down his face and onto his chest. He couldn't remember how many wounds he'd sustained. Pain screamed through his left shoulder; his right knee felt far too weak. When would it give out? Sweat streaked into his eyes, stinging, and blurring his vision. His muscles burned from overuse. Countless bouts before this, he'd bested his opponent in under three rounds. Never had he worked so hard for a victory. His body ached, but he defended himself, for it was all he could do.

For Cecilia.

Too deep on the defensive, he couldn't regain his strength. *Damn, I'm in trouble.* "Enough," he called and hoped his voice held.

"Pathetic, Lethbridge," Ulstead said with a snarl. "Your father would be disappointed." Then the round-ending blow came without the bigger man acknowledging his concession like a gentleman. "You're done, and don't you ever attempt to threaten me again. Miss Dawson was too weak a woman for me." His opponent kicked Lewis' bad knee, and as pain went through his leg, he slammed a ham-fist into Lewis' stomach that lifted him off his feet and sent him flying over the grass.

He landed hard on his back with a knee on fire, and bent while gasping for air. Unfortunately, he had no strength to regain his footing even though his mind screamed at him to stand.

"Shit." As if he were disconnected from himself, he laid there while life continued around him. The judge came near with the doctor, and he counted down from ten while Lewis didn't move in the sweet meadow grasses, wheezing and mentally cataloging his injuries. Sometimes, a man had to take the loss, but he didn't have to like it.

At least I'm not dead.

The crowd roared as Ulstead was declared the winner. At the start, Lewis had been the favorite, unless one counted the betting books at various clubs. Now, he'd fallen from grace, and what a bitter tumble it was. To the man who'd allegedly took out his frustrations on a woman.

I'm sorry, Papa.

"Lewis!" The wild concern in Cecilia's cry stabbed through his chest.

Lewis sat up in time to catch the other man's bloody grin, and he nodded. "Good show, Ulstead. You bested me soundly." The fight had been a much-needed challenge and changed the way he thought of himself. Perhaps he wasn't the prize fighter he'd thought, and because he'd lost the prize purse, he was even less of a catch than even his mother would admit.

What the devil do I do now?

As a few of the more rabid fans of the sport swarmed Ulstead's corner, Lewis struggled to his feet and returned to his. Once there, he accepted a towel from Alexander. He hated to face a potential lecture from his brother, but there was nothing for it. He'd been an embarrassment out there.

"That wasn't your best performance," Alexander murmured, but instead of the disappointment in the other man's eyes, there was speculation and a bit of worry.

"I know." Over Alexander's shoulder, his gaze connected with Cecilia's. Shock reflected on her face. Her blue eyes were wide and round and held way too many questions, but nowhere could he discern disgust. That only gave him a modicum of relief.

"You were distracted."

"I *know.*" Lewis wiped at the blood and sweat on his face and head. "My shoulder is done for." To say nothing about his knee. Then he drew the towel over his chest. "It won't happen again."

Alex snorted. "You'll be dead with another time in the ring."

"You had him routed at one point," Duncan added, "but like Alex, I think you had other things on your mind."

"Perhaps." He shrugged, and when his muscles screamed a protest, he groaned.

"I don't know what to say, but at this rate, you'll go bankrupt soon." Alex tossed Lewis his clothing. "Get dressed. No sense lingering about. Your fans have deserted you."

"I don't need your censure right now." After another pass of the rag over his face, Lewis threw it into the empty water bucket with the others.

"No, but we *will* talk soon." Instead of chastising him further, Alexander asked, "Do you require medical assistance?"

"Nothing is broken, save my nose and my pride." He yanked on his garments. "I'm in no mood for company."

"Too bad, because we are all riding back to Town together. You can sulk in the coach." Alexander flicked his gaze around the immediate area. "I'll leave you alone for a few moments before we leave. Come, Duncan."

Lewis rolled his eyes. "Subtle, brother."

"Perhaps you'll have more skill at courtship than at boxing." Alexander glanced at Duncan, who shrugged and retrieved the bucket. "If you're so tied up in knots now, I can't imagine what you'll be like given another few weeks."

"It's not… I'm not… There isn't…" He stopped talking, for his brothers weren't listening. They exited the ring at the opposite side.

Eventually, the crowd thinned. Ulstead held court with a small knot of supporters at the far end of the meadow. Bastards who withheld their appreciation when things went bad. With a sigh and a tight chest, Lewis ducked under the rope and approached Cecilia. What was there to say? He'd failed.

Spectacularly.

"You were wonderful out there," Cecilia said in a soft voice. Her gaze roved over his chest, and she bit her lower lip slightly as she stared. Awareness tingled through him. "I had no idea watching a boxing match would be so heart-pounding, so exciting, so real."

Bloody, bloody hell.

"It is, uh, raw. I'll give you that." He yanked a linen shirt over his head, shoved his arms into the sleeves, and then smoothed the garment over his torso. Damn, but his shoulder ached. The admiration sparkling in her eyes nearly saw him undone. What he wouldn't give to kiss her right now, to take refuge in those eyes. "Thank you, but I lost."

"That doesn't matter, because you survived. Isn't that the most important lesson?"

"Not when I was depending on that prize purse."

She pressed her lips together and peered around him. "While I'd hoped you would have beat *that man,* seeing you pound your fists into him was quite satisfying." Slight hero worship reflected in her eyes. "I rather enjoyed both watching you and hoping he might come away with a broken bone or two."

"Ah." Unable to help himself, Lewis chuckled, and then groaned because it hurt too much. "I've no doubt given him a few bruised ribs. Sorry I couldn't do better."

"What you did was quite enough." She laid a hand on his arm. "I am proud of you."

As his chest tightened, Lewis fought off the emotion rising in his throat. "Thank you. That means so much." The words were choked and said in a low voice. "I'm glad you were here." If there weren't so damned many people about, he might have taken her into his arms and kissed her. "I like having my brothers with me, but each time I glimpsed you, my spirits rose." Not enough to win, apparently.

A blush stained her cheeks. "Do stop, Lethbridge. Of course I would support you. Why wouldn't I come out for my boxing instructor?"

Was that *all* he wanted to be to her? It required more thought, and much more talking to her... about himself. "Come. We should head back to London so I can lick my wounds in private."

"You have nothing to be ashamed about, but I would caution you to rest the arm and perhaps put a salve on the knee."

It was rather nice to have someone fuss over him. "As long as I'm not stiff and confined to my bed tomorrow, instead of a lesson tomorrow, I will take you driving. As per my promise to Alexander." After today, after seeing the man who'd beat her take absolutely no responsibility for what he'd done, Lewis wanted the right to protect her from everyone else.

A genuine smile was his reward, and it was worth every blow he'd received today. "I would enjoy that very much."

Oddly, so would he.

Chapter Eight

June 26, 1817

IT HAD BEEN two days since Cecilia had watched Lewis go up against her former fiancé in an illegal boxing bout, and while he had been breathtaking in his element, she had also enjoyed sitting beside him in an open carriage, spending time with him in a capacity that had nothing to do with fisticuffs.

For once, the rain had stopped, and the sun made an appearance. The day was warm and finally summer-like. She turned her head and peered at the earl from around the shallow brim of her straw bonnet. "Thank you for doing this, Lewis. It has been an age since I have been escorted about in society."

"It is, of course, my pleasure." When he met her gaze, the bruises were evident on his face when the sun hit his skin. "You deserve to be treated like a princess." When he offered a grin, flutters went through her lower belly. "That color, that lovely, ethereal light blue, on you makes you fairly glow."

"Oh, what a lovely thing to say." It had been a long time indeed since she'd been complimented by a man. But then, if she were speaking of her fiancé, after the first six months of the engagement, all those words had run false. "My father always makes sure that I have gowns and dresses for every occasion, but I rarely go anywhere to justify his expense."

"Any man worth his salt who loves a woman will do his best

to see her cared for regardless of the relationship."

She nodded. Still, the dress of periwinkle lawn trimmed with dark blue ribbons made her feel quite feminine and let her pretend that she was tall and slim like the popular women currently in fashion within the *ton*. "He hopes I'll make a good match. To be honest, I think he is worried about my future, but I can take of myself."

"Let him worry. He is your father, and speaking from someone who has lost his father, you only have him in your life for a specific time." Emotion graveled his voice. "Good or bad, let him be your father."

It was the most personal tidbit she'd had from him since they'd begun their relationship as instructor and student. "Thank you for the reminder."

He guided the pair of horses with a steady hand. Though the horses weren't matched, they were still beautiful equines—one a bay mare and the other bay with white dappling throughout. Clearly, his skill with the ribbons meant the horses obeyed his veriest command.

Several moments went by as he guided the carriage through a spate of traffic as they approached Rotten Row which ran along the southern side of Hyde Park. The silence between them was of the companionable sort, and she didn't mind it, for there was no tension there. Cecilia was perfectly content to remain beside him, watching the world go by while catching subtle whiffs of his shaving soap. And through it all, she couldn't quite ignore the fact that her right shoulder brushed his left each time he moved, reminding him of the solid strength he carried.

Eventually, the earl stirred. "Mr. Ulstead is a real bounder," he said as he kept his gaze focused on one of the horses. "He said you deserved everything you got, and for that reason alone, I wanted to beat the stuffing out of him during the bout. In that moment, the money didn't matter."

"Oh." She was glad the man hadn't seen her at the bout. Just knowing he was there had sent fear crashing down her spine.

"For what it's worth, I'm glad you gave him your best. I wish I'd had the courage to fight back years ago, but I wasn't strong enough."

"You are working to reverse that, though."

"Yes, but that doesn't mean I want to come face-to-face with that man again," she said in a quiet voice. "Being with Mr. Ulstead was one of the worst experiences of my life." Clenching her gloved fingers in her lap, she sighed and frowned at the horses. "While knowing him stole my trust and confidence in men, it also showed me exactly what I don't want from a relationship. Yet..."

"Yet?"

Another sigh escaped. "How can I know a man is true when so many lie in the beginning to lull me into complacency?"

"The good ones have no need to lie."

She snorted. "The ability to discern the difference between the good ones and the bad ones is quite difficult, and is a skill I apparently don't have."

As the earl navigated the vehicle onto Rotten Row, he glanced at her. "Sometimes, I think, you must trust what fate wishes to bring you."

"Is that what you practice when it comes to matters of the heart?" Suddenly, she wanted to know everything about him, including how many women he'd been with in the past. Not that she had a claim to him or his time.

"I don't know that my heart has been engaged by a woman before." A muscle in his cheek ticced. "Had them in my bed? Yes, of course. I am not a monk, but to be honest with you, I haven't been with a woman for at least six months."

"Oh? Why?" She'd not thought of him as a rogue or a man who would go from bed to bed, but he was easy on the eyes and an earl, so surely, he would be much in demand.

When he shrugged, his shoulder brushed hers, but he winced, a clear indication that he was still in a bit of pain. "I suppose it didn't appeal to me after realizing just what a mess my father had left me in with the properties and nearly empty title."

"That is understandable, but it's a bit sad as well. Aren't you lonely?"

He snorted. "Are you?"

"Touche." But the conversation tugged a grin from her. "Is falling in love and eventual marriage something that interests you?"

"According to my mother, I'm to marry or at least find myself engaged by the end of the year. Preferably to an heiress in order to do my duty to my title." In his huffed out breath, she heard the frustration and strain he must labor under. "I rather think she doesn't care if I'm in love or not, and honestly, I have to wonder how often titled men are afforded the luxury of love or even romance."

"That is such a sad way of looking at the world." A squeeze of sympathy went about her heart. If she harbored the hope that he might wish to indeed court her with marriage in mind, that was dashed, for she wasn't an heiress even if her father had promised a sizable dowry. "Everyone should experience the feeling of falling in love at least once in their life."

He glanced once more at her, and when their gazes connected, he said, "Even if the relationship doesn't work or proves disappointing with heartbreak?"

Another point for him. "Yes, even still, because when we allow ourselves to feel everything, we know we're alive. If we keep ourselves aloof from all that, what is the point of living?"

"Very true." The earl nodded, but his gaze had dropped to her mouth, and his eyes were more green than brown in that moment. "You are wise, Lia. I appreciate that. Far too many women of my acquaintance simply parrot back my own views to me. That isn't helpful."

"I would imagine not."

Another long stretch of silence was shared between them, broken by the rhythmic rumbling of the wheels on the road as well as the horses' hooves striking pebbles in the dirt, various calls from some of Lewis' acquaintances, and the general buzz of conversation and laughter the closer they came to the jam of carriages all vying for space on the thoroughfare. It was one of the most pleasant afternoons she'd passed in recent days.

Eventually, he broke the silence. "Where would you like to go now? An ice at Gunter's? It's a bit late to visit the British Museum, but I don't mind going for a whirlwind visit."

"Honestly, when I go there, I'd rather have time to look at all the exhibits. Perhaps you can drive me over to my father's shipping office? I need to collect the most recent invoices and the ledger book so I can do some work at home. Papa doesn't want me at the office by myself any longer."

"I must agree with him. Until I know you can land a full-grown man on the ground with a well-timed punch, it's best to keep you safe."

"Ha!" She half-turned toward him and in the process, her knee crashed into his. Heated tingles went up her leg to lodge between her thighs. "I knocked you on your arse, didn't I?"

His lips twitched with the beginnings of a grin. "You were lucky, and I was distracted."

"Liar." Be that as it may, it still counted. "I'll practice much more diligently now."

"I have no doubts."

Cecilia kept her own counsel for the remainder of the drive over to the docks.

Chapter Nine

AN HOUR LATER, as she unlocked the door and let them both into the building, she said, "My father has three meetings on his schedule this afternoon, but has promised to be home for dinner by eight."

"And your brother?" the earl asked as he prowled about the downstairs office, poking into various shelves and nooks while she closed and locked the door behind him. His gaze went over the closed Venetian blinds as well as the shade drawn to hide the window glass on the door, but he said nothing.

She shrugged. "He has his lessons with tutors. In a few days he's due to spend a month with a friend at that boy's father's country estate. It will be a relief not having to worry over him for a bit."

"What is upstairs?"

"A small apartment where we lived before Papa's business started doing well, which allowed us to move to Mayfair." Carefully, Cecilia put a stack of envelopes as well as already opened invoices on top of the leatherbound ledger book and rested it all on the corner of her father's desk. "Would you like to see it?" She led the way to the back room where they could access the narrow wooden staircase.

"Of course." He stood aside and gestured for her to proceed

him. "When did the move occur?"

That small consideration and nicety left her breathless for a couple of seconds. "Uh, perhaps a couple of years before James was born. It was already cramped quarters and would have been trying to have a baby in the mix, but I remember Papa being so proud he could provide an actual townhouse for us all."

Their footsteps echoed on the treads, but as soon as she unlocked the door and let them both into the living space, the nostalgia and comfort of being transported back to a time of security assailed her. A time before she'd known how ugly and horrid life could be.

"Don't mind the dust covers. We took some of the furniture with us to the new house. If there is much work for Papa or he wants to meet ships coming in after-hours, he will sometimes sleep here."

"Well, it is quite convenient."

"Yes." It was hard to breathe with him so close and his big presence filling the space. Being alone with him like this was much different than being alone with him in the boxing salon, quite possibly because she was in skirts.

But what difference did that make?

On that second level, aside from the common room—or parlor—there was a small kitchen with a stove for boiling a kettle or perhaps warming a stew or soup, and there were two bedchambers on the floor above. She tried to imagine what the earl thought of the simple living space, but it proved a difficult task, for he kept his own counsel, and his expression remained inscrutable.

Needing something to occupy her instead of standing about watching him like some sort of moony schoolgirl, Cecilia went to the windows in the parlor and opened the draperies. "Our housekeeper comes in once a week to tidy and dust."

"Ah." When Lewis joined her at the window, she trembled at his close proximity.

"When I was a girl, I used to stand at these windows and

watch the ships in the harbor, both leaving and arriving. But my favorite ships were the ones embarking on adventures. I tried to imagine where they were going when they reached the open waters and all the wonderful things those sailors would see."

"Is adventure what you want, Lia?" The inquiry was asked in such a low voice she had to strain to hear. "Or are you a woman who can find adventure wherever you are?"

"I haven't given that much thought over the years." She turned to regard him, and nearly tumbled into the green-brown pools of his intense eyes. Why did it feel as if she were on a precipice, wondering which way she might fall? From his own admission, he needed to marry, and if she wasn't a suitable candidate, he needed to leave her in peace. Heated, consuming kisses aside, she refused to be relegated to a mistress while he made someone else legitimate. "What do *you* want, Your Lordship?"

"I… No one has ever asked that of me before." For long moments he stared at her as shock followed by admiration reflected in his eyes. Then, he nodded. "Honestly? It's you, Cecilia. In this moment, I want *you*."

Gooseflesh raced over her skin. "Oh?" Her heart beat out a rapid tattoo while she struggled to puzzle out his true intent.

"I can't think about my future, but I know that I want you in this moment."

It was perhaps the most honest he'd been with her, for raw emotions left his voice graveled. "I appreciate your frankness."

"I have found no purpose for dancing around an issue." A muscle in his cheek ticced. "However, I can understand if my words have shocked you. After all, we have known each other but a week."

"And yet have shared some very intimate kisses." She quirked an eyebrow. "Either you have felt something for me or you were only using me to amuse yourself." It made all the difference to determine which.

"I would never hurt you, Lia." He rubbed a hand along his

jaw that was shadowed with light stubble. "Surely, you've felt the attraction, the desire, between us?"

"I have." She might be on the shelf as her father had said, but there *were* proprieties, and she refused to fall victim to a man again. "Such things are highly scandalous. I grow tired of only being wanted as either a punching bag or a convenient place for a man to stick his wick." If her words were vulgar, so be it. They were true, and as he'd said, there was no use dancing about an issue.

"I adore how outspoken you are… or have grown since we met." When the earl cast a glance about the parlor and then returned his gaze to her, a gleam had entered his eyes. "We are quite alone with no one scheduled to interrupt us…" He grinned, and her heart fluttered.

You are naught but a silly widgeon, Ceci.

"I…" What did it say about her character that she wanted him as much as he allegedly did her? "I am not a fast woman." Wary and desperate, perhaps, but not fast.

"No, you are not, and if things grow out of hand or you find yourself frightened, you are quite skilled in drilling a knee into a man's privates."

She snickered. "It is the quickest way to elude an attacker."

"True." When his expression shifted and reflected wicked hopefulness, the rest of her resistance crumbled. Before she could offer up a protest, he scooped her up into his arms, chuckling when she squealed. "From the first day you walked into my boxing salon in that wretched disguise, I have wished to explore every inch of your body."

"Such gammon." She snorted in derision, but at the same time, there *was* something romantic about being in a man's hold as he carried her across the room to one of the low sofas. "Was it such a terrible disguise, then?"

"To me, yes."

"Yet we have known each other a handful of days."

"There is an invisible connection between us that has bedeviled me from the first. Why else do you think I kissed you during our second lesson?"

"Only after I kissed you first."

"Another truth." He had barely released her, let her feet find purchase on the floor before he tugged her onto the sofa with him. "You're certain you wish to do this? There might be certain consequences...."

"Hush, Lewis." Cecilia smiled even as the reality sent cold apprehension into her stomach. She tugged at his cravat. "I know my own mind and accept whatever fate gives me." Then another thought occurred to her. How would he react to the fact that she wasn't an innocent? Would he consider her soiled goods?

"You are a brave woman; I've never met anyone quite like you."

"Such pretty words you use, yet you claim your brothers are more charming." She knew next to nothing about him, but she couldn't shake the feeling that he needed her somehow, over and above the physical sense.

"I have my moments." After removing her bonnet and letting it drop to the floor, he held her head between his large hands, stared into her eyes and then he claimed her lips in a gentle kiss that managed to both steal her breath and ignite tiny fires in her blood.

Immediately, Cecilia was lost to the tide of sensations he invoked within her. She looped her arms about his shoulders— oh, they were so broad and muscled!—and sought to kiss him back, and when that familiar meeting of mouths wasn't enough, she sighed against his lips. "Show me in no uncertain terms how much you want me."

"I think you've gained far too much confidence with your lessons." Yet he dragged his lips down the side of her throat. When he reached the crook of her shoulder, he nibbled and licked her skin while tangling one hand into the mass of her hair. Pins fell to the hardwood with tiny *pings*.

"Whose fault is that, Your Lordship?" she barely managed to

mention as shivering pleasure spiraled along her spine.

"Indeed, I'll take full responsibility." With a few yanks and tugs, he had her dress up and off her body. The petticoat, stays, and shift soon followed, then there was truly nowhere she could hide from his intense regard. "Better than what I imagined," he whispered, and still he caressed and touched her skin until her bones held the strength of cooked porridge.

"Oh!" She toppled backward against the bolstered end of the sofa, and he followed, came over her body as if giving her pleasure was his only purpose in life. Breasts, nipples, ribcage, navel, mons, nothing escaped his attention.

And, dear heavens, it was so different from sharing intercourse with her former fiancé.

When she thought he'd leave off to undress, he didn't. Instead, he explored her body with hands and lips. Lewis encouraged her to bend one leg at the knee so he could press featherweighted kisses to the inside of her trembling thigh. The slight scrape of his stubble created another layer of delight, and she lost the ability to breathe. When he moved on to her other thigh, Cecilia shook from anticipation and need.

Every time she reached for him, he batted her hands away. "Lewis, please!" The man was quite vexing.

"This is your first time; I want you to enjoy it without the distraction of worrying over my pleasure."

"I..." She forced a swallow into her suddenly dry throat. "Before we go further, I should confess I am not an innocent."

"What?" For a few fleeting seconds, he looked at her in confusion.

"Years ago, I let my fiancé bed me. I thought if I did, he might stop beating me..." Saying the words aloud didn't portray her in the best light, but there was nothing for it. "However, he was much more skilled in beatings." A sheen of tears rose into her eyes.

"Damn."

"If you wish to stop—"

"No." The earl shook his head. "Even in this, you deserve so much more than you have been given, and I can assure you, I am *not* like him." And he was once again over her, his fully clothed body covering hers… protecting her. The drag of the fabric over her sensitive nipples made her catch her breath; the cold press of the buttons on his jacket to her belly elicited a sigh of pure appreciation.

"Lewis…" She couldn't remember what she wished to say, for this was simply lovely.

"Let me do this, let me show you how women *should* be treated."

A snort escaped her. "Even if this is highly scandalous?"

"That is quite subjective, my girl." He claimed her mouth with such drugging kisses that her mind spun. All thoughts vanished beneath a haze of passion. Over and over, he drank from her, and when he probed the seam of her lips with the tip of his tongue, she gladly opened, inviting him in.

The feeling of falling assailed her despite her reserve and her wariness; he was different, and it surprised her.

Dueling with his tongue slowly replaced sparring with him as one of her favorite things. There was simply nothing quite like the slide of silk against satin, and with each pass, heat seeped into her veins. Every time he chased her tongue, she imagined him thrusting into her with a very different part of himself.

"Even in this you are a quick learner," he whispered against her lips.

"Mmm, I must have a good teacher." Was there a limit to how long one could be kissed? Cecilia didn't know, but she gave as good as she got, let him teach her the finer points so she could mimic what he did, and as always, it wasn't the slobbery, off-putting affair her fiancé had shown her. All the while, she plucked at the buttons of his jacket, because she needed to see him.

Every last naked inch of him.

"Please let me—"

"Not yet." He encouraged her arms over her head, and with

his lips against the underside of her jaw, said, "I have other plans for you just now."

Hadn't he already explored her body, bedeviled her with kisses designed to tease and arouse? When he eased a hand between her thighs, her legs shook. Still bent at the knees, they provided a cradle for him to rest, and as he stroked his fingers along her folds from top to bottom, a sigh of pleasure escaped her. "Oh!"

"I'll take that as permission to continue." And he continued to tease her. Every time he slipped those talented fingers downward, he dipped one of them into her passage. "Ready so soon?"

"Do hush, Lethbridge." Unable to do anything else, she attempted to regulate her shallow breathing and keep her eyes open, but whenever one of those digits invaded her channel, she sucked in a surprised breath. "If you wish to play, do it, but stop tormenting me."

"That is half the fun, Lia." The earl then parted her flesh and encouraged her swollen nubbin out of hiding. She gasped. The touch of his fingers and the application of various degrees of friction quickly sent her hurtling toward a glimmering *something* she'd never experienced before. "Lewis, I… I…"

"Your fiancé was a blooming idiot if he didn't put in the time to make you spend."

"I won't argue with you." Further words fell out of her desire-soaked brain, for with every pass and circulation to that tiny bundle of nerves, she felt as if she'd jolt out of her skin. Dear heavens, how was she to survive such titillation?

It took next to no time for her whole world to revolve around the heated kisses he continued to give her and the insistent strum of his fingers on that little button at her center. Bands of pressure built and stacked low within her belly. Though Cecilia writhed beneath him, he didn't leave off with his torture.

"What are you doing to me?" Her words came out stilted and choked in a whisper.

"It's quite all right if you fly. That is the point, after all." His breath steamed the shell of her ear; the weight of him pressed her into the brocade cushions of the sofa.

"But, I..." She scrabbled for purchase as the sweet torture went on, and then, quite suddenly, her whole body stiffened. A wave of bliss crashed into her, and she succumbed to it. He truly did send her flying, or rather, pinwheeling into the heavens. Shivers went through her body, tickled into her nerve endings as she shook with the release.

"That certainly didn't happen the last time," she finally managed to gasp out when sanity returned. Her body felt lethargic, yet restless hunger remained. "I hadn't thought..."

His chuckle reverberated in her chest. "I am not nearly done." Lewis eased off her, and as she watched, he divested himself of every stitch of clothing he wore.

Oh, finally!

If she'd thought him beautiful stripped to his waist for that bare-knuckled fight, his naked form was quite spectacular. Lean and muscled in all the right places, his belly and abdomen flat and slightly ridged. Toned thighs set off his erect member perfectly, and not even the various bruises and scrapes that decorated his skin could detract from the vision of him. "I wish I could paint." As he joined her again, she stroked a hand along his abdomen, and when the muscles contracted beneath her fingers, her mind drifted to all the naughty places she'd like to visit with him.

On him.

Oh, how she wanted to play! The notion surprised her because she'd assumed she wouldn't want anything like that with a man again.

"Even with the bruises you still find me attractive?" he asked as he took her into his arms once more and reacquainted himself with the crook of her shoulder.

Heat went through her cheeks as tingles danced down her spine. "Attraction doesn't merely stop at someone's physical looks. You are so much more than that."

"Ah, Lia. Somehow, I think life is about to grow far more

complicated than I thought."

"There are worse things…" The hard, hot length of him twitched insistently against her thigh. Trembles went through her muscles, so she distracted herself by exploring his back, his shoulders, his chest, glancing her lips over his bruised and battered flesh. The scent that clung to his skin was intoxicating. She kissed as many parts of him as she could before he once more took possession of her lips with a kiss of his own.

"What will you do when you can't box any longer?"

His body went taut. "I honestly don't know, but if I keep having poor showings like you saw a couple of days ago, my career will be over long before my body breaks." His voice was tight, rough with emotion.

"Sometimes life isn't about winning, Lewis. It is about trying, fighting, getting up when you fall."

"Perhaps, unless one needs the coin." He kissed her again, preventing further discourse, and as he settled himself more comfortably between her splayed thighs, the tip of his member bumped her opening.

Tingles of need cascaded down her spine and tightened her nipples. Feeling daring, Cecilia slipped a hand between them to cup his equipage. This was so much better than anything she could have imagined. His hiss of surprise echoed in the room, and wishing to experiment, she gave him a gentle squeeze. "I wish we had more time so I could investigate this properly." Did that make her sound like a wanton?

"I'm going to spend prematurely." He chuckled but removed her hand from his person. "It's been far too long for extended play."

Had their boxing relationship enhanced those feelings? The primal feel of his body pressed into hers as well as the throb of need deep in her core whisked everything she wanted to say out of her mind. "Then you shouldn't wait any longer." She wrapped her legs around his, and when she slid one of her hands down his back to squeeze a buttock, he groaned and ground his hips into hers. "Claim me, Lewis. Show me I'm not making a mistake."

"You aren't." Concern warred with desire in his voice. He put a hand beneath her hip, and then with one powerful thrust, he penetrated her body and didn't stop until she was fully impaled. Then he paused, found her gaze with his. "Damn."

"I agree." Being completely claimed by this man she'd known only a week, the man who patiently taught her how to punch and defend herself... Well, it was beautiful. Tears stung her eyes, and she quickly blinked them away. Once she'd wriggled beneath him and into a more comfortable position, she gave him a nod. "I like this. It is so different from that last time."

"So it should be." He grinned and she was at sixes and sevens from the wickedness in that gesture. "The right man does make a difference." Then he moved, slowly in and out of her passage, and every push and pull gave her different layers of friction and pleasure. "Lift your hips each time I stroke into you. That will help you find a rhythm more quickly."

"Oh, goodness!" How lovely was the press and surge of two bodies coming together in the most ancient of ways. Pleasure threatened to drown her. With her feet flat on the sofa, she was better able to meet his thrusts, and all too soon the slap of flesh against flesh echoed in the room, punctuated by their sighs and moans. "Lewis, I need more."

"So do I." Then the beat changed. The earl dug his fingers into her hip, as he pistoned ever faster while he moved his other hand to one of her breasts. "I'm not going to last."

Deeper. Harder. Shorter. Each stroke demanded her full attention.

"You are so lovely." She peered into his face. Such intense concentration held his expression, and then she didn't care. Every time he speared into her, that familiar pressure mounted, bigger and bigger, until finally, she shattered again, and the surprise of that second pinwheel into bliss provoked a keening cry that she didn't bother to try and stifle.

As contractions rocked Cecilia's core, the earl thrust once

more. He immediately followed her into that void full of white light and velvety nothingness. His member pulsed. The warmth spreading through her passage solidified the intimacy of the act. When her fiancé had come, it had been traumatic, and he'd left right after. Tears escaped onto her cheeks, for this had been like nothing she'd ever experienced before.

Seconds later, Lewis collapsed on top of her, and his weight further worked to bring her closer to him. She wrapped her arms around him, holding his head to hers while her heartbeat hammered, and her breath rasped, and she shivered back into reality.

"I don't know what to say," she admitted in a shocked whisper.

"I'll wager that is a first." The earl rolled onto his side, taking her with him, then he held her in his embrace while she listened to the strong, fast beat of his heart. "I'm glad I could share this with you, but if something should come of this coupling, I—"

"No." Interrupting with a shake of her head, she interrupted him. "I don't know if I want a man permanently in my life, but I *do* know I don't want one out of obligation for any reason."

What they had shared in this moment was enough. He hadn't promised the future, and she never demanded it. Things were complicated for them both, and perhaps their paths would go in different ways once their lessons concluded.

"But—"

"Hush, Lethbridge. Don't ruin this." She bussed his cheek. "We can work out any frustrations in the salon with the sandbags." For now, she basked in the glory of being bedded by a man who knew what he was doing, and it had been everything she'd dreamed it would be. "But perhaps we shouldn't repeat this until we can both puzzle out a few things regarding our lives."

He nodded, and once more nuzzled the crook of her shoulder. "Agreed, yet this isn't the end of our relationship, Lia. It can't be."

Only time would tell.

Chapter Ten

June 28, 1817

IT HAD BEEN two days since he'd apparently lost his mind and had bedded Cecilia, and in those two days, she'd been all he could think about to the detriment of keeping appointments and missing the occasional meal.

What the hell is happening to me?

That coupling had been more than merely a physical joining. It had been full of humor and teasing, both emotional and a bit freeing as well. If put to the test, he'd admit he hadn't had that sort of a connection with a woman before, and even days later, it had the power to stun him. But she was one of his students and he was her instructor. That sort of thing couldn't be allowed to happen again.

Could it?

"Lewis. Is all well?"

The dulcet sound of Cecilia's voice yanked him from the thoughts. He frowned as he glanced at her while holding the reins of his open carriage. "Uh, yes, of course. Merely woolgathering, I suppose."

She nodded. "There is much to think about."

"Yes." Since the day was once again sunny, he hadn't wished to remain inside giving her a lesson locked away in his office, so he'd sent a note 'round to her townhouse asking her to dress as she usually would and that he would take her driving in the afternoon. "Are you enjoying yourself?" Should he refer to what happened between them two days ago or was that bad form?

Beyond that, what did it mean for their relationship, and for that matter, were they beyond student and teacher or friends even if they were still strangers to each other?

"I am. Parts of London are beautiful in early summer before the air gets stale and the pollution and stench becomes overwhelming."

To that end, would she like to accompany his family to their country estate in Kent? For that matter, did his mother plan to remove there for the summer? His brothers might not wish to leave the salon for that long, and frankly, he didn't blame them.

"One of my favorite places in Town is Hyde Park at this time of year. Sometimes, when the sunlight slants over the Serpentine just right, it seems as if a million diamonds sparkle over the surface of the water. Combined with the whisper of the breeze in the tree leaves, I can truly forget I'm in London entirely."

"And in those fleeting moments, you can pretend you are not an earl with multiple responsibilities hanging about your neck," she added in a soft voice. "I understand the sentiment completely. There are times when I think about running away and starting my life over somewhere far removed from here."

He couldn't help but frown. "You aren't happy?"

"Most of the time I am." When she shrugged, her shoulder rubbed against his arm, and the quick jolt of heated response caught him off-guard. "However, I have to wonder what my purpose is. Everyone else seems to have something to occupy their time that might work toward the greater good, but what am I doing? Keeping the books for my father's shipping business? I'm not even a wife or a mother, nor are there charities or causes that have captured my fancy."

He pressed his lips together. "Do you envision yourself being a wife and a mother?"

For the space of a few heartbeats, she remained silent. Then she sighed. "I did when I was younger. It was all I could think about, almost that it was a longing inside me that if it didn't happen, I might die."

"And now?" She had such an interesting way of describing things, and it continued to draw him toward her.

"Now, I will be content if I found a man who doesn't beat me, who can see something in me beyond the shape of my body, who will wish to grow old with me, not for what I can do for him, but what we can achieve together." When she glanced at him, sadness reflected in the blue depths of her eyes. "After what I have seen of men, I don't know if any of that is possible."

Her ability to show herself in a candid light stunned him and reminded him that he needed to show vulnerability to her at some point so they could connect more deeply. "I would like to hope I am showing you that not all men are as the bounders you have described."

The soft laugh that escaped her throat sent heated awareness dancing over his skin. "Let us just say that I am constantly surprised by you."

At least there was that. "Is working for a cause something you're interested in?"

"I don't know. I haven't given it a thought, and I've not had spare time that needs filling." She focused her gaze on the horses. "Of course, I'm not a highborn lady with loads of leisure, so perhaps I needn't worry about it."

"I have a few charities I'm a patron for, but I can't tell you how long it's been since I visited any of them personally." Cold disappointment in himself coiled through his chest. "That was something my father was so much better at than I. It was one of the reasons he liked boxing. He always said it helped him connect with people not of his own class, and that the salt of the earth as well as personal satisfaction was found in the regular people who populated London, not with the rich." He blew out a breath of frustration. "In this, I'm afraid I've failed. One of many things my father would lecture me on."

For one fleeting moment, she laid a gloved hand on his thigh, and he thought he might jump out of his skin. "You haven't failed, Lewis. Just because you don't do things as your father did them, that doesn't mean your way is the wrong one."

Some of the rising anxiety was quelled by her words. "Thank you." The longer he sat beside her in that carriage, the more he craved that calm, that… peace. Did being with him give her that same feeling? In many ways, he hoped so. "My life has been quite turbulent since my father passed two years ago. It was sudden and none of us were prepared for it. Additionally, there was no time to tell him goodbye."

Why he thought now to tell her a bit about his past, he couldn't say, only that it felt right.

"That was how it was when my mother died." Her voice caught. "She perished while giving birth to my brother. It was all very hushed and harried; I was with tutors but when I finished, my father told me she was gone. Something like that leaves a person stunned and in shock, sometimes angry, without a way to work through the emotions."

"Which was one of the reasons I enjoy boxing, or at least I did until the persistent injuries detract from that." How long would it be before he took one too many punches and couldn't function any longer?

"I quite like sparring for that," she said with a wobbly grin. "There is something satisfying about drilling my fist into yours, and I want to explore that even further."

"That is something I understand as well. The feel of it, the sound of it. Of course, we will continue to put that in your lessons." He nodded. "Yes, on many levels, all the components of boxing keep emotions in check."

"Or ignored." Again, she rested her hand on his thigh. "You can't continue going through daily life without acknowledging how you feel, and there is nothing wrong with that. Showing your feelings doesn't mean you're weak."

"If I'm being honest, Lia, it is a struggle. Daily." Suddenly, he knew exactly which path he wanted to tread, at least for the next few months. It wasn't something he could explain but he wished to explore, and that would require time. "I need to ask you something."

"All right."

After pulling the carriage over beneath a bridge within Hyde Park, he held the reins tight in one hand and then turned toward her on the bench. "I am well aware you and I don't know each other all that well, but there is enough trust built between us in the boxing salon to allow for familiarity."

"To say nothing of the scandal we got up to at my father's office a couple days ago," she added in a droll voice with amusement dancing in her eyes.

"There is that." A grin tugged at the corners of his mouth. "To that end, I enjoy spending time with you, and…" He forced a hard swallow into his throat. "I… I wish to pay my addresses to you if you're of the same mind."

Clearly, I'm well on my way to madness. That was the only explanation.

She frowned. "If this is out of some misguided honor because we coupled, I—"

"It's not," he hastened to interrupt. "You made your views quite clear on that the other day." For a few moments, he regarded her. "This is purely because I want to know you better, and we can't go around Town without having at least a reason, else the gossips will cut us both to ribbons. Hell, they probably already are, for both times I've taken you driving, we haven't had a chaperone or at the very least a maid with us."

And he didn't care.

"Yes, and my father will ring a peal over my head when he hears of those incidents. No doubt after this, we'll be stuck with a maid."

"I won't mind. Though I wish it would be your brother."

"James is with a friend for the next month."

"I look forward to meeting him. Your brother can tell me all the secrets you wish to hide. Besides, I want the boy to learn how to defend himself. It will serve him well as he goes through life."

"Oh, Lewis." With a sigh, she fixed her gaze on her hands in her lap. "Paying your addresses to me is a large commitment with an inherent promise involved. I rather doubt I am a woman of whom your mother will approve."

In truth, his mother would no doubt offer up a large protest, but he couldn't worry about that right now. "My mother isn't the one who will spend a potential lifetime with the woman I choose." Shock tightened his chest from the admission. "So, do I have your permission? I don't wish to force myself into a situation in which I'm not wanted." Surely courting couldn't be as easy as being in Cecilia's company.

"I…"

"Lia, look at me." When she didn't, he put curled gloved fingers beneath her chin and raised her head until their gazes connected. "If you can't envision a possible future with a man like me—"

"Stop, Lethbridge." The smile she gave him was rather on the watery side. "You are a good man, but you are also an earl. While most women would climb over their friends or shove them down for a chance to catch a titled man's notice, I'll be the first to warn you away."

"Why? I don't understand."

She heaved a sigh. "I am a captain's daughter… the daughter of a merchant and definitely not the heiress you should be putting your interest upon."

"None of that matters to me. I have full confidence in my boxing skills to bring in coin to fill the Stapleton coffers, which gives me freedom in *this* matter."

"Well, you *are* easy on the eyes, especially when you are boxing," she said with a laugh that immediately had his spirits rising.

"I'll have you know, there is much more to me than looks." He couldn't help but chuckle. "Except now, since the bruises haven't faded all the way."

"Are you fishing for compliments?"

"Is it working?" Bantering with her was something he thoroughly enjoyed.

"I refuse to inflate your ego." But she smiled, and he had difficulties breathing.

"Right." If he wasn't careful, he'd give in to the urge to take her into his arms and kiss the hell out of her. "Is your father at his office this afternoon?"

"He might be. Though I keep his books, I'm often not privy to the whole of his schedule." Then she frowned. "Did you wish to meet him?"

"I think I should, especially in light of the new arrangement you and I have discussed." Once he took up the reins again, he set the carriage into motion. "I don't want him to think I'm doing anything underhanded with you."

She touched his arm. "As I have said before, you are a good man. He will be happy to meet you."

During the trip to the East India Dock, they talked of many things but mostly focused on his relationship with his brothers as well as his mother. Though it was slightly difficult to answer her questions—after all, this was the most chatting about himself he'd ever done with anyone outside his relatives—oddly, he wanted her able to understand him better.

After arrival, he tossed the reins to a boy outside the mews, gave him a coin and promised another upon retrieval, then he offered Cecilia his crooked arm and led her along the boardwalk while watching the activity on the harbor.

They were one building away from her father's when a large hulking man stepped out from an alley, and when he caught sight of Cecilia, he shouted at them to stop.

"Unhand the woman; she's mine." One of his beefy hands curled into a fist.

"I beg your pardon? You must have us confused with other people." As he spoke, Lewis tucked her behind his back and put his body between her and the brute.

"Miss Dawson will be my wife soon, so leave her alone." He took a few steps toward them, and Lewis straightened his spine.

"Don't listen to him, Lewis. Mr. Derrickson is the man who continually accosts me, the reason why I'm taking boxing lessons in the first place." A trace of fear threaded through her whispered voice. "He is the one who forces kisses on me."

"Ah." This man required a lesson. "I am the Earl of Lethbridge, and if you know what's good for you, you'll step away and leave this woman in peace."

"The last time I checked, I ain't beholden to Mayfair nobs." He cracked the knuckles of one hand. "And this ain't the place for you. Leave Miss Dawson here and I won't dirty up your mug more than it already is."

"Is that a threat, Mr. Derrickson?"

"What if it is?"

"Then I'll have no choice than to follow through on my order that you leave her alone."

"Once I clean your clock, you won't be able to keep her from me." Then the bigger man pounced. He took hold of Lewis' arm and then threw him away from where Cecilia stood.

After a few stumbling steps, Lewis regained his balance and recovered from his surprise. "You'll pay for that." He followed the threat with a sharp uppercut that caught Mr. Derrickson on the chin.

The bigger man staggered backward, but with a roar, he came back at Lewis with a vengeance. Quickly, he landed a punch into Lewis' stomach that had him doubling over, and took full advantage by curling a fist into the back of his superfine jacket and attempting to throw him into the harbor.

"Lewis!"

Barely did Cecilia's shout of warning register in his brain, but Lewis quickly wrenched himself out of the other man's hold. Scuttling around the barrel-chested man, he put the sole of his boot to the back of one of the man's knees and shoved. That put

Mr. Derrickson off balance and brought him awkwardly kneeling on the boardwalk. Before his opponent could recover, Lewis landed a blow to the side of his head that sent him sprawling onto his back.

"Leave Miss Dawson alone or I'll come back and finish you off," he said, in between wheezing breaths.

"Buggar off." Mr. Derrickson rubbed the side of his face and glared. "I'd better not catch you around the docks again. I'll kill you the next time."

"Doubtful." Lewis snorted as he glanced at Cecilia, who watched him with concern evident in her expression. "I'm a prize fighter, friend. Engaging me further in fisticuffs will not go well for you."

"I know who you are, Stapleton. And rumor has it that you lost your last bout." The bigger man scrambled slowly to his feet. "I'm better than you. Get me in the ring and decide. Winner gets Miss Dawson."

"That can be arranged." Lewis winced as his left shoulder throbbed with pain.

"Enough, the both of you. I am not a prize to be won." Cecilia rushed between them before they could come to blows once more. With a gloved palm to Lewis' chest, she glared at him. "Come. Now is not the time to linger here." Then she narrowed her gaze at Mr. Derrickson. "I have told you more than once that I want nothing to do with you. Perhaps this time my words will penetrate through your thick skull. Leave me alone, or I'll let Lord Lethbridge beat you bloody and be happy to watch."

"You can't escape me forever, Miss Dawson," the other man said with a snarl. "Once you're my wife, I'll keep you away from all other men."

"Firstly, I don't belong to you, Mr. Derrickson, And secondly, women are not objects nor are they slaves. They still have free will even if they choose to wed, but the key here is choice." She narrowed her eyes and encompassed them both in her gaze. "You will never be that to me." Then she shoved at Lewis' shoulder and nudged him back down the boardwalk toward the mews.

He grunted but meekly walked at her side. "I could have put that man down with enough authority that he wouldn't bother you again."

"Don't be more of a nodcock than you can help," she responded in a waspish tone. "Mr. Derrickson is a dunce with more brawn than brains. You are better in every conceivable way, but you need to learn discretion." A frown took possession of her mouth as she glanced at him, and all he wanted to do was kiss her from her defense. "Do you hurt? I have a feeling your shoulder pains you. I could see it in your face when you threw that last punch."

"A bit." How could he deny it? She was much too observant.

A huff escaped her. "Why couldn't you just let it go? You could have ignored him instead of engaging in a fight."

Couldn't she understand that he did it for her? "That man dared to touch you; he insulted your honor. It is my duty to demand satisfaction." Was he truly this far gone over a woman already? Ever since he'd met her, he'd felt at sixes and sevens. Today was no different.

Perhaps that was a good thing, for it was much like embarking on an adventure.

"Just like I told him, I am not an object to be owned. I am a woman who knows her own mind, so if you wish to be with me, you must stop this penchant for possession." Again, she looked at him, the emotions in her eyes inscrutable. "I enjoy your company, Lewis, and I appreciate your defense, but you need to know I can fight my own battles."

"While I understand that, if we are to embark upon a relationship, you need to know that you don't have to any longer. I want to be your partner, where we share every burden and work through every problem. Together." God, where did that thought come from?

Am I truly going to court this woman?

When she glanced at him again, shock reflected on her face.

"Truly?"

"Yes." There was no going back from this moment. "I am a man of my word." Even still, he wanted the right to protect her, because that was what women deserved anyway while maintaining their own agency.

Slowly, she nodded and then slipped her hand through his crooked elbow even though he hissed in pain for it was his left arm. "Then my answer is a tentative yes. You can pay your addresses to me, and I look forward to seeing what comes of that." Then she grinned, and he temporarily lost the ability to think. "You can talk to Papa later. For now, let's get you to the salon. You need a salve rubbed into your arm and your knee. Someone needs to look after you since you refuse to do that for yourself."

Lewis couldn't argue with her about that, and in this moment, he was glad to have her in his life. *Please help me to not cock this up.*

Chapter Eleven

June 29, 1817
No. 12 Balsam Court
Manchester Square
Mayfair, London

"WHERE ARE YOU off to this morning, Ceci? To the lending library? The bookshop? You seem quite happy, wherever you're going."

Cecilia smiled and looked up as her father came into the morning room where she was enjoying toast with marmalade and a pot of strong tea. "Good morning." She dabbed at the corners of her mouth with a linen napkin. "I am off for sparring lessons with Lord Lethbridge."

"Ah." He filled his own teacup and then sat beside her at the table. "The mysterious earl." One of his eyebrows rose in question. "The same man gossip is flying about for being seen squiring an unknown woman about twice in the last week. Was that you?"

Heat filled her cheeks. "Most likely." Thank goodness James hadn't yet risen for the day. "I know you want to lecture me on the folly of such a thing, of not taking a maid with me, and I understand that. However," she blew out a breath, "I am seven and twenty, Papa. Not an innocent deb, and neither am I starry-eyed or naïve. I can take care of myself, especially now."

"I didn't accuse you of being any of those things." Her father took a sip of his tea. "However, I am going to caution you to be careful. The both of you don't need shredded reputations."

"Honestly, Papa, I don't think the earl cares about things like that. For a titled gentleman, he isn't snobbish or arrogant." She spread marmalade on a triangle of toast as she thought over her next words. "He isn't one of those men who reminds you of who he is. I appreciate that."

"I've heard that about him, which is the exact opposite of what his father was like." He continued to sip his tea as he regarded her with speculation in his eyes. "Lethbridge's father made the mistake of having his whole identity tied up in his title and the wealth therein. Unfortunately, he became a bit too fond of the gaming tables."

"I assume he didn't have skill there?" From everything she'd gleaned from conversations with Lewis, she knew his father had all but bankrupted the family.

"He did not." A chuckle came from her father. "But he always thought he could restore what he'd lost through winning boxing bouts." He shrugged. "Yes, the man's real talent lay in fisticuffs, but when that all came to a stunning, abrupt end, where did he leave his family?"

"In a mess, which the current earl is trying to rectify." For that, he had her admiration. "I might not know the whole of his history, but keeping his family name in good graces with the *beau monde* and keeping them together is what drives him."

"Which means he is an honorable man who won't put you into danger or treat you badly."

"No, he won't," she agreed in a low voice. "The earl is different from anyone I have ever met, Papa." Heat popped into her cheeks. "In fact, yesterday he asked if he could pay his addresses to me."

"Oh?" Surprise propelled that one word into being. "What did you tell him? Ever since your disastrous engagement, you have been adamant that you didn't want another man in your life."

"I know, and I did think that. Perhaps still do, deep down." She frowned at her piece of toast. "Yet there is something about the earl that has captivated me a bit, and despite my reserves and distrust, I would like to see how this might unfold." As she met his gaze again, she offered a smile. "With your preliminary blessing?"

"I haven't seen Lethbridge for many years. However, I did know his father and he is a decent boxer." He slowly nodded. "I will allow this, but eventually, he will need to come here and talk with me. Until then, play by the *ton's* rules as much as you can, else gossip will bury the two of you, and I have a feeling a forced engagement won't sit well with either of you."

"You're right." Fighting off another round of heat in her cheeks, Cecilia ate her piece of toast and then chased it down with some tea. "Which is why I'm meeting Lewis in Hyde Park this early. Not many people will be around to witness our sparring, and it's a fat lot better than sneaking into the boxing salon while wearing a disguise."

"That it is." He nodded and then stood. "I wish you luck, and I'm glad you are not content to stand around waiting for life to happen to you. Some of the men on the docks are crude; they're greater threats than the earl, I'll wager."

"Yes." She kept her own council on the blows exchanged between Lewis and Mr. Derrickson yesterday. "He won't hurt me, Papa." Though, if her father knew the extent that her fiancé had beaten her or that he'd essentially raped her... Well, he'd never let her out of the house. Tears filled her eyes, and she quickly blinked them away. "For whatever reason, I am coming to trust the earl."

"That's good, but I still wish to meet him, so I can see for myself." He leaned down and bussed her cheek. "You are my only daughter. I can't help but wish to protect you."

"I will let him know your intentions." She took refuge behind the rim of her teacup. "I should be home around midday."

"Enjoy yourself, and if you bring the earl home, I don't want you alone in the same room with him. You are a beautiful young woman," he said with a wink.

Another round of heat went through her cheeks, for she had already been quite scandalous with said man. "I'll call for my maid. You have my promise."

"Very well." He nodded, took his folded newspaper and then strode to the door. "I'm at the office should you have need of me."

A few flutters went through her belly, for she couldn't wait to see what the day would bring. After all, this was the first day the earl would officially start courting her.

"I'M ANXIOUS TO start. I've wanted to get back to sparring since that first time." The spot in Hyde Park the earl had chosen was quite remote and set back within the trees. Somehow, he'd found a small clearing of grass near a thin, gurgling stream.

"When you knocked me on my arse?" Since he'd already stripped to navy breeches and a fine lawn shirt, she only needed to remove her bonnet and spencer.

"Yes." As she roved her gaze over his chest while he rolled the sleeves of his shirt up to his elbows, heat came over her. What she wouldn't give to see him bare chested instead. "It wasn't my fault you were distracted."

Would that happen again this morning?

"True. I challenge you to see if you can do that again." When he sent her a grin, a push of heat went into her cheeks.

"What if I don't want to strike you again?"

"That *is* the gist of boxing. Besides, when you tagged me the last time, you didn't cause pain."

"Then I shall need to do a better job this time, but I promise to avoid your left shoulder." That caused her considerable worry anyway. When she blew out a breath, a curl ruffled on her forehead. Though she'd put her hair in a braid and pinned it about her head like a coronet, there was no breeze, which made the air a bit stifling.

"Don't think about that; your attacker that you might face won't give you the same consideration." Lewis tugged a pair of worn, brown leather gloves—mittens—from the bag he'd brought. "Put these on."

"They really are quite ugly." Once she held them, she wrinkled her nose. "And they stink."

"Many men wear them in the salon, and since we aren't attending tea, you'll survive." Lewis snorted with laughter. "How is your father this morning?" He slipped on a matching pair of gloves, pulled the laces tight with his fingers and teeth where needed.

She wished she was that coordinated. "He is well, but as expected, he wants to meet you." With a grunt, Cecilia tugged on the padded mittens. "Especially when I told him of your wish to pay your addresses to me."

"Does he think me good enough for you?" Apprehension darkened his eyes.

It was adorable seeing his vulnerability. "He is hopeful, I think, and protective."

"Well, he *is* your father."

"These gloves are tighter than the ones from the other day. I can barely curl my fingers."

"Perhaps I grabbed the wrong size, but many pairs were in use this morning. The padding will prevent serious injury."

"Then why use them?"

"I don't wish to hurt you. This is a training scenario only, not a scene where we beat each other to a pulp."

Worry flitted through her mind. "I don't want to hurt you."

"You won't, so ignore the thought." Command rolled in his voice. "You're letting fear overrule your common sense." He came forward, closing the short distance, and dropped his gloved hands on her shoulders. "Concentrate on the lesson. You've done well so far. Don't let fear be the bully, else you'll lose the fight from within, and I know you are not the sort of woman to let anyone control you."

"I am not." She grinned. "Not even you."

"As it should be. Now, fists at the ready. Knees slightly bent. Keep your muscles loose. Remember to circle your opponent—me."

"Will you tag me first?"

"Come at me and we'll both find out together. Since this is sparring, we *will* exchange blows." He gestured with his padded fists and then assumed the position. "Give me your all, and I'll do the same. Within reason, of course."

"Right." She smacked her gloved hands together. "No mercy, Lethbridge."

"I shouldn't think so. Think of me as Mr. Derrickson."

She made a gagging sound. "You are a hundred times better than him. More handsome, too." As Cecilia planted her feet, she lifted her fists, and leaned forward slightly. "He won't give up, you know."

"And neither will I relax my protection of you." He gently tagged one of her mittens with his, setting them both into motion by circling her. "You hesitated too long, so I took the advantage. No distractions, remember."

"Not fair." But she circled him, watched him. Then, she struck, threw a punch… that missed his upraised fist. Both of them. "Drat."

"Sometimes, patience is your best bet. Have you been doing that?"

Cecilia snorted. "Not recently. There have been other… activities to hold my interest."

A dark flush rushed up his neck and into his cheeks. "Fair enough, but the people who would beat us down or bully us will never play fair, which is why you've asked me to teach you to box. Lead with your knuckles and trust yourself." Again, he tapped her gloved hand with his and darted away. "Come at me."

"You won't like it."

"Neither will you if I need to defend, but it is my hope you'll grow to love the sport."

"I am already fairly engaged with it, so we are on the right path." Cecilia circled him while keeping her mittened fists raised.

Each time he threw a punch, he connected lightly with her hands. When he returned to a guarded stance, she swung. The first few missed him, and he retreated, which made her concentrate that much more. Truly, boxing was more than using one's fists.

"Why can I not punch you? I did it with ease the last time we sparred." Frustration rang in her tone. When she lashed out with what should have been an uppercut, she only grazed the tip of his mitten.

"Because last time you were trying to prove something to me." Lewis held up a hand. "Now, you've either grown lax or your concentration is not on me as your opponent or on boxing in general." When she frowned, he blew out a breath. "What has you distracted? And I will not be amused if you say me."

She snorted. "You are not, at least not in *that* way."

Much.

"Oh, thank you." Sarcasm lingered in his voice. "Are you worried about your brother or your father?"

The corners of her lips twitched, but she didn't fully smile. "No."

He cocked an eyebrow. "What, then?" He propped one mittened hand on his hip, which only served to call her attention to that part of him. "Let's have it out in the open so we can move forward."

"It *is* you I'm worried about." She stepped forward and shoved at his shoulder. "Do you have any more illegal bouts scheduled?"

"I do not, but if a boxer drops out and I'm offered the chance, I will take it."

"For the coin." It wasn't a question.

"Yes. I have responsibilities."

"So do your brothers. They are helping the family coffers as best they can."

"I'm the head of the family now; it falls on me." He huffed as he stared at her. "It is my burden to carry. Not yours."

"Perhaps a week ago it was, but not now." She propped her mittened fists on her hips, which had his gaze jogging down her body, leaving heated tingles behind. "You and I are… partners. And we were since you decided to court me. When I'm in trouble, I hope you'll help—which you have. The same goes for you. I'm not going anywhere, Lewis, but I don't want you to put yourself into a position where you might be seriously hurt, which might affect your future."

"I understand." His eyes rounded and surprise reflected in those green-brown depths. "It's flattering, for I've never had anyone in my life who wished to see to my protection."

"The man in a relationship is not required to do it all, and he isn't supposed to be the strong one all the time." Her chin quivered and a sheen of tears rose into her eyes. "You treat me with respect, and I do the same for you. If we don't trust each other, this relationship won't work."

Wasn't that the point of sparring also?

"You are quite something," he said with a slight grin that put flutters into her belly.

"As are you." Cecilia pressed her lips together. "Agreed?"

"Fine." He nodded. "Finish this lesson, this sparring, and we'll talk about our courtship." Putting space between them, he raised his glove-covered fists. "Of all the women in London, I had to find myself involved with the most stubborn."

"Ha!" She resumed the stance for a fight. "I have simply learned to fight back, to fight for the life I want," she said with a wobbly smile, for there wasn't anywhere else in the world she wanted to be in this moment.

"I'm proud of you, for you have come a long way since that first day you came into my salon." Lewis stepped forward and rested a mitten-covered hand on her shoulder. She tilted her chin up so their gazes met. "Keep making a stand. It's an attractive quality."

"Oh?" Immediately, her expression brightened.

"You have a backbone and spirit. Decent men appreciate that." He stepped away. "Use your difficulties and challenges as your fuel."

For long moments, they circled each other over the soft early summer grass. Then she gasped. "I just realized what I want to do with my life soon."

"And what would that be?"

"Teach other women to fight so they can fight off attackers of their own. You might not be able to teach them because of society's views, but I can. Or we can together if we had a private salon." Another gasp, for she was rushing her fences. They might not suit for a lifetime. "Er, I mean, perhaps. I just enjoy boxing so much," she rushed to add, when his eyebrows soared.

"You are amazing, Lia. I'm damned glad I met you." Though he said nothing about the future, he didn't need to. The bemused expression on his face spoke volumes.

And her confidence soared. She again raised her hands. "Shall we begin?"

"I rather think we already have." When he raised his fists, he flashed a grin. "If need be, think of me as the man who perpetuated your reason for boxing lessons, the person you wish to pummel into the ground." He circled her. "Come at me with vigor this time." Then his eyes took on a faraway look. Was he woolgathering?

It didn't matter. His distraction was her opening, so she tagged his shoulder, which brought his attention to her face.

"Damn! Good show!"

"Ha!" Cecilia again raised her fists, her gaze never leaving his. "Stand and deliver, Lethbridge. Next time, I'll find my mark on your handsome face."

"And add to my bruises?"

"Unless you defend yourself."

He snorted. "Confidence is the first step to outsmarting your opponent." Once more he circled her, and it was an odd sort of dancing, this bobbing, weaving, constantly moving over the grass.

"You are a lovely teacher." And if she wasn't careful, she might fall for him before her head was ready. Then, she darted into his space, and when she threw a punch, it connected with his left fist. The smack of leather against leather resounded in the air, as did his groan. "I'm sorry."

"Never apologize during sparring. Keep going," Lewis encouraged in a soft voice.

"There is a certain thrill to this sport, a rush of excitement, and an immediate disposal of everything unpleasant in one's mind as soon as my fist connects."

"Yes! That is exactly it." He gestured at her with a glove. "Punch me again."

"All right."

As she gained more confidence in her stance and the power she wielded with her fists, her punches connected more solidly with his gloves. Occasionally, Lewis would swing and tap her hands or tag her shoulders, but she quickly learned how best to defend herself, when to retreat, how to rout him and set him on the defensive.

"You are doing well; I'm in awe of how you've taken to the sport."

"I'm merely studying you." She emulated him, watched his feet, bounced her gaze between his fists each time he jabbed or lunged, then she made the same work for her. "And it is lovely exercise."

As the lesson continued, sweat dampened her back and made her cotton dress and shift stick to her skin. Sweaty tendrils of hair clung to her temples, and each time she delivered a punch, she grunted. Her jabs connected more solidly so that she felt them whenever she found her mark.

And it was quite thrilling.

Then the sparring intensified. The tip of her glove glanced over his cheek, and when she voiced concern, he came roaring back, his glove skimming her shoulder. With a huff, she delivered a jab that caught him in the breadbasket—she thought that was what it was called—and left him temporarily winded.

"Nicely done." Then Lewis struck out and landed a soft blow to her other shoulder, which spun her about.

"Oh… you!" Cecilia came back like a wet cat. She pummeled his fists with enough force that he stepped backward a few times as she advanced. He tagged the shell of her ear, so she gave him a jab to the temple.

"Had you been a man with bare knuckles, that would have sent me to my knees.

Admiration rang in his voice.

"Not bad from a woman, hmm?"

"Again, I'm proud of you."

And they continued to spar in the clearing.

"Is that the best you have, Lia?" The taunting in his voice annoyed her as he wiped at the sweat on his forehead with a sleeve.

"You tell me." Before he was ready, Cecilia got off a punch to his chin, though gloved, that sent him reeling backward until he toppled over onto his back.

For the second time in their acquaintance during sparring.

"Yes!" With a grin, she put a foot on his chest. "You've been down for more than three seconds, Lethbridge. Does that mean I've won this bout?"

His grin was quite cheeky. "That is exactly what it means." His voice was still winded.

The giddiness in her chest couldn't be contained. She stepped away and gave a little jump for joy. "You didn't let me win?"

"I did not." He moved his jaw around. "There's a bit of pain there because that was a fantastic punch." The longer he looked at her with admiration and pride, the warmer she grew. "Our next lesson should be quite interesting."

"Will we box with bare knuckles?"

"No." He snorted, and when she offered him a gloved hand, he grasped it and together they levered him to his feet. "I don't want your hands bruised or your knuckles bloodied."

"Oh."

"However, there is something I wish to ask you." When she cocked an eyebrow, waiting, he sighed and worked at removing his mittens. "My mother is throwing a summer ball in a handful of days. Will you attend as my guest?"

Cecilia stared at him. "You want me to come to a ball with you?" Did she even have a suitable gown?

"I would, yes. You can meet my mother and perhaps dance with my brothers." He shrugged. "It is my hope you will rub along well with my family. For obvious reasons." There was an intensity in his eyes that sent tingles of need down her spine.

It was a huge step, and one that caused her a decent amount of trepidation, but she nodded and held out her hands so he could help her out of the mittens. "I would adore that. Thank you." After clearing her throat, she asked, "What if your mother deems me not good enough for you?"

"Then I will tell her all the reasons why she is wrong… or I can put you both into a boxing ring at the salon and let you spar it out."

"Don't you dare!"

He chuckled as he removed her second glove. "All will be well. Don't worry." With a soft growl, the earl tugged her into his arms and set out to apparently kiss her senseless. Afterward, when they were both breathless, he grinned. "Ah, Lia, life has become quite interesting since I met you. I don't know how to think about that."

"Perhaps you shouldn't question fate, hmm." But she smiled as she retrieved her mittens from the ground. There was no doubt now; she was becoming rather more fond of him than what was probably good for her.

So why was she steeling herself for something bad to happen?

Chapter Twelve

June 30, 1817
Stapleton House
Marylebone, Mayfair
London, England

L EWIS STARED OUT one of the windows in the drawing room, for once more he and his brother intended to have dinner at their club tonight, but if he were honest, he wished he could spend that time in Cecilia's company.

And that knowledge left him at sixes and sevens.

"What the devil ails you, Lethbridge?"

The annoyance in his brother Alexander's voice made him frown. Slowly, he turned about to face the man. "What do you mean?"

"I've asked you a question two times, and you've ignored me." He crossed the room to the sideboard, and once there, held up the decanter of brandy with an eyebrow raised in question.

Lewis nodded. "I beg your pardon. It seems I'm falling into woolgathering more frequently these days."

"Ah." The clink of crystal on crystal rang in the air as his brother poured out two glasses of the amber-colored liquor. "In other words, your brain is being eaten up by a woman."

Before Lewis had the opportunity to respond, Duncan came into the room. Clearly, he'd caught the end of the comment, for he hooted with laughter.

"You could be correct, Alex. Current gossip indicates our dear earl has been seen in the company of a woman not of the *beau monde*."

Heat creeped up the back of his neck. "Is that so?"

"Get off it, man. I'm one of those people who saw you out driving with her," Duncan continued with a laugh. "And unless I miss my guess, the mystery woman is Miss Dawson, the woman you've been giving boxing lessons to." One of his eyebrows rose. "Am I right?"

Was there any point in lying? If anyone within society could ferret out secrets, it was his youngest brother. "You are." As soon as he accepted the glass of brandy from Alexander, he took a large swallow and welcomed the burn in his throat. He might as well admit to it and tell them how it came about lest they contribute to the gossip. "About a week after the lessons started, I decided that I might wish to pay her my addresses."

Both brothers wore matching expressions of shock.

It was Duncan who spoke first. "Why? She isn't titled, nor is she an heiress."

"Why should that be the only thing to recommend her?"

"Of course they shouldn't but—"

"He apparently finds her interesting," Alex interrupted as he deposited himself into a chair. "And to be fair, she's a looker. Got enough curves to tempt a saint."

Heated annoyance rose in Lewis' chest. He took refuge in taking another swallow of brandy. "That is not your concern." If he were honest with himself, he didn't want his brothers leering at Cecilia.

Alex ignored him to focus on Duncan, who was pouring out his own glass of brandy. "I'll wager he's bedded her and that has put a maggot in his brain, making him think he has a responsibility toward her."

"If it were me, I would have taken her to bed from the first introduction," Duncan said with a cavalier shrug as he came near with his glass. "I mean, those lips alone are enough to reduce a man to a puddle. Imagine them wrapped around my c—"

"That's enough!" Lewis' roar echoed in the sudden silence of the room. He refused to have the image of Cecilia with either of his brothers. "Lia is *not* up for discussion."

"Lia, is it?" Alex's eyebrows soared into his hairline. "Now *that* is a good indication the two of you are rather more intimate than you're letting on."

He fought off another round of embarrassed heat. After a sip of brandy, Lewis blew out a breath. "I am not discussing any of that with you."

Duncan hooted with laughter. "He's bedded her." When he lifted his glass, he shot Alexander a knowing look. "Cheers, brother."

"God, the two of you are insufferable." After finishing his own brandy, Lewis set the glass on a small round table nearby. Then he moved back to the window. "What Miss Dawson and I do is our own business. Drop the subject."

"Oh, but we can't do that." Of course Duncan would pursue it. He was like a dog with a bone. "For years you've evaded any sort of attachment. Even before Papa died, you took mistresses, but when he left this mortal coil, it was almost as if you retreated into yourself, and you took no notice of anything. Now we hear that you're paying your addresses to a woman you are supposed to only be teaching boxing to? You did this to yourself."

"I quite agree," Alex said with a nod. "Especially because you promised Mama that you would seek out an heiress at the very least."

"Actually, no." Lewis blew out a breath. "I promised her I would *think* about finding an eligible woman, not that I would make inroads into it." Why did this conversation make him so angry? Did he secretly think his family would prove disappointed in Cecilia? Perhaps that was it, and he rather hoped she would make a good impression. "Regardless, Miss Dawson is a solid choice. She is a captain's daughter, and from what she's told me, there is a fair dowry on her head. Additionally, she is clever, intelligent, humorous, and quite down to earth."

"Who is?"

As if the evening couldn't get worse, his mother came into the drawing room with curiosity stamped through her expression.

Lewis rubbed a hand along the side of his face. "Miss Cecilia Dawson."

She frowned. "I don't recognize the name. Who are her people?"

He cast a glance at his brothers. Both of who grinned like the idiots they were. Clearly, no help would come from that quarter. Then he heaved a sigh. "She is the daughter of Captain Dawson. He runs a shipping outfit where we source some of the things we need in the boxing salon." The muscles in his gut pulled tight. How would his mother react?

As his mother sat on one of the low sofas, she arranged her skirting about her legs. "Why are you boys talking about her?"

"Well, Mama, because Lewis has decided to pay his addresses to her." Duncan shot him a sly look as he sat beside her. "This is significant, because when was the last time he showed any interest in a woman beyond anything fleeting?"

Surprise jumped into her eyes as she pinned him with her gaze. "This Miss Dawson is the woman you are courting?"

Since the floor didn't swallow him whole, Lewis nodded. "She is. I've already spent more than a week with her, and everything I am learning about her has impressed me. I asked a few days ago if I could pay my addresses to her, and she gave permission."

Duncan's grin was this side of cheeky. "He has also been giving her boxing lessons."

"Oh, Lewis." His mother's lips curved into a frown. "She's *that* sort of woman?"

Hot annoyance flared once more in his chest. "What sort, Mama? The kind who wishes to protect herself from bounders and rogues? The kind who is tired of being molested by unwanted attention from men?"

Alex snorted with laughter from his position across the low table. "To be fair, Miss Dawson has quite the talent for fisticuffs."

"So then your whole relationship thus far is steeped and rooted in scandal." It wasn't a question as she continued to frown at him. "Is this your way of having revenge on me for demanding that you marry?"

Bloody hell.

"Of course not." How did life become such hell all of a sudden? "In fact, I had no intention of doing anything with her except teach her how to box." He turned to the window and stared unseeing out of the glass, went so far as to open one of the panels and let a bit of fresh air into the room. "After spending time with Miss Dawson, however, she and I became friends."

"And then some," Duncan interrupted with another chuckle.

Damn the man's eyes.

Lewis ignored him. "There is something about her that has impressed the hell out of me. She's from good stock; the captain is a pillar in society, and from all accounts, he and his daughter are issued many invitations throughout the year."

"Yet she isn't an heiress." This was also not a question. His mother shook her head. "You know how desperately we need an influx of coin to prevent an interruption of our lifestyle."

"I am aware, of course, but the captain is offering a sizable dowry." With a sigh, he turned to face her. "I don't know the exact number, but then, I am nowhere near making an offer for the woman. We have only just begun a courtship of sorts."

Was that even what their relationship could be called at this point? Lovers, surely, but was she his mistress or merely a friend? It was too complicated for further reflection just now.

"Regardless of the number, it likely won't be enough." She waved away his comment. "She's not even from a titled family."

"No, she isn't, but that doesn't make her incompatible." When did his family become a group of snobs? Had they always been like this, or was it merely the stress of looming financial difficulties that brought it out? "Miss Dawson is a lovely woman."

"Have you met her father?" His mother narrowed her eyes. "You were raised within society's rules, Lewis, and it seems as if you are doing your level best to break every one of them." Before he could speak, she continued. "You might think I'm immune to gossip, but I have heard the most recent rumors. Imagine my surprise when they weren't about Duncan this time."

The disappointment in her eyes nearly leveled him. But he wasn't about to go down without a fight. "Of course I've lived my life by rules; I couldn't escape them as the eldest son. My life has been mapped out for me since birth. Hell, I wasn't allowed to serve in the military like Alex or Duncan because of the damned responsibility of the title." Ordinarily, that wouldn't bother him. That was simply how life was, but for whatever reason, the thought that his mother—or his brothers—would reject Cecilia merely on her pedigree soured him to his core. "However, your dictate to me was to find an eligible woman. I believe I have done that, and what is more, I'm intrigued by her. Why isn't that enough?"

"Because it is your responsibility to make this family solvent again." At least she didn't dance about the issue. "You know that."

Some of the anger he'd always had to tamp down came rising to the surface in a heated, strong wave, and this time he couldn't contain it. "Except *I* wasn't the one who put us all in this position to begin with!" With the roar, he encompassed his family in his gaze. "As much as we all loved Papa, he had his problems and struggles. The man was addicted to gambling and got in over his head, but not one of us stepped in to stop him."

Duncan frowned. "How could we? He wouldn't have listened in any event."

"We don't know that. It's all assumption at this point." Shaking his head, Lewis moved toward the grouping of furniture. "Regardless, we are all left with the mess he made, me especially. I understand that my holding the title now leaves me responsible for all of you, but damn, it's a difficult truth to swallow." He bounced his gaze between his brothers. "I love the both of you, but you need to step up and help as well. It's your name that might hit the gutter just as much as it is mine."

"Haven't we done that by fighting in bouts?" Alex asked, with doubt reflecting in his eyes. "We are doing our best."

"With love, no you are not." His pulse rushed so hard in his ears he wondered if they could hear the wild beat of his heart. "Duncan spends coin indiscriminately, always thinking I'll be able to pay his creditors with each new invoice." When he leveled his attention on his youngest brother, the man paled slightly. "I'm cutting you off; should have done it months ago, but I'd hoped you might change your ways knowing what we faced."

"But—"

"No." Lewis chopped the air with a hand. "The decision is final. If you want pocket money, if you want to continue to pay for your rooms at The Albany, you find a way to do it yourself. I'm done aiding your careless lifestyle. You will need to figure out how to make a living."

"We have the boxing salon. I am content with taking the reins of running the business if you promise to let me experiment with new things and different sorts of lessons."

It was a large ask, and without being in control, the salon might flounder, yet at some point, he needed to trust that his brothers would do the right thing. Hadn't he learned that from Cecilia's strength and determination? "Very well. I'll step back from the salon, and will only conduct lessons if they are privately booked. I will also pay you a salary. Is that acceptable?"

"Yes." A light of interest lit Duncan's eyes. "Have your man-of-affairs put it in writing so we can both sign it."

"I will." With every word he uttered, a degree of calm crept in to steal some of his anger. Perhaps all he'd needed to do was stand up for himself. None of it was unreasonable. "I can't do this alone, and truly appreciate the assistance." Then he looked at Alexander. "You are not as wasteful as Duncan, and you live here.

I don't mind that and would never pitch you into the gutter. However, as the second son, I *am* asking that you find a way of making a private income to alleviate some of the strain. I understand that you keep the books for the salon, but I also know you despise it. I can easily find someone else, but unless you start bringing in a financial contribution, I will be forced to sell some of our holdings."

"I appreciate the honesty." Alex nodded. "Yes, please find someone else to do the accounting. I'm rubbish at it and much prefer to enter into bouts for coin even though I'm not as skilled as you or Duncan." Then he heaved a sigh. "But I promise to find something interesting I can use to generate funding."

"Good." With a nod of gratitude, Lewis drew in a deep breath and let it ease out slowly. "We make a decent team, and I think that together we will see our way through this."

The silence in the room was overwhelming as all three of them stared at him.

Yet his confidence continued to build. Pride in himself rose. What would Cecilia say once he told her of the stand he'd made? Then he moved toward his mother, sat on her other side on the sofa. "You must trust that I'm capable of making the right decisions for my own life. One of those decisions is going forward with a courtship of Miss Dawson. If she isn't what you envisioned for me, so be it, but it isn't as if I'm going to ask for her hand tomorrow. We are nowhere near that." He forced a swallow into his suddenly tight throat. "However, I refuse to marry and not have love. I can't imagine being leg-shackled to a woman with whom I can't share every aspect of my life with. Not even for you."

A sheen of tears made her eyes luminous, but she nodded and rested a palm against his cheek. "I've only wanted the best for you, for all my sons." With a nod, she gave him a tremulous smile. "And I want you to find happiness, Lewis. I know none of this is fair to you, but consider who you are aligning yourself with. The woman you take to wife needs to be strong, for she will not only be your countess, but she will need to contend with everything society will throw at her. I'm not certain that a woman not raised within those sorts of strictures will make a wise choice for you."

Fair enough, but the words sent doubt twisting down his spine. "Let me worry about that, hmm? In the meantime, the boys and I are late for the club." Good God, but he needed to be out of the house and away from the unrelenting pressure for a time.

"Of course." When she rose to her feet, the three of them scrambled to theirs. "I will talk to you tomorrow."

As she left the room, Lewis heaved a sigh. "Shall I ring for the carriage?"

Duncan nodded. "Yes, but I have a bit of news you might find of interest."

"Oh?" He strode across the room and then yanked at the blue velvet bell pull. "What is it?"

"There is a bout to be held in three days. One of the prize fighters fell ill and had to withdraw from consideration. The organizer dropped by the salon yesterday and asked if I could convince you to stand in."

"The same night as Mama's ball?"

"So it appears."

Damn, she would be livid if he ducked out early, but the call of earning coin was strong. "Who will I fight against?"

His brother shrugged. "The man's name is Derrickson. Don't know his Christian name, but he's apparently an emerging name in the bare-knuckle community in a greater weight and strength than you. Brings in big numbers of spectators which means the prize purse is always large."

Bloody, bloody hell. That was the name of the man who continued to bully Cecilia at the docks. Hadn't he said he was a boxer the other day? "I'll do it," he said without thinking. "Perhaps I'll make a better showing in front of Lia than my last bout."

And this was personal.

Alex frowned as he joined them at the door. "What of your shoulder? You still favor it."

"It will always be an issue, but I need to do this out of principle." His brothers didn't need to know why. "Tell the organizer I'm in."

And he would hope for the best, in all aspects of his life.

Chapter Thirteen

July 1, 1817
Stapleton House
Marylebone, Mayfair
London, England

DEAR HEAVENS. *I think I'm going to retch.*

This morning, a courier had come to the house with an invitation to join the Countess of Lethbridge for tea that afternoon. There had been no reason or explanation given, just the invitation, and now, as she followed the butler up a wide marble staircase, she couldn't help the flutters of anxiety that bounced around in her belly.

Why does Lewis' mother want to see me?

Perhaps Lewis had told her of his courtship and now his mother wished to contend it?

There was no way of knowing.

At the drawing room doors, the butler paused. "Miss Dawson is here to join you for tea, Your Ladyship," he said in a tone that sent a bit of a chill down her spine.

"Lovely, show her in, Garrison." Though the countess' voice had a cheerful ring to it, that didn't alleviate the worry gripping Cecilia's stomach.

When the butler moved aside, he gestured her into the room. "I'll order your tea now."

"Thank you." The countess nodded, though her gaze was fixed firmly on Cecilia. "Welcome to my home. I'm so glad you accepted my invitation."

She was a lovely woman whose features put her in mind of each of her three sons. They all took after her in some way. Her brown hair had been arranged in an upswept style, and in the sunlight streaming in through the open windows, strands of silver glimmered in her tresses. Her gown of robin's egg blue satin gave her face youthful color and life. When she smiled, fine lines framed her mouth and crinkled the delicate skin at the corners of her eyes, but by and large, she was a handsome woman for her age.

A masculine chuckle tugged Cecilia's attention to the other occupant of the room, Lord Wexley, Lewis' middle brother. "I rather think you didn't give her the choice, Mama." He nodded at her. "Good afternoon, Miss Dawson. It is good to see you again."

Though having a familiar presence there brought her a modicum of calm, he didn't prevent her nerves from being felt strung too tight. "Hullo, Lord Wexley. It's lovely to see you as well." She glanced at the countess, who waved her into a chair. "Thank you for the invitation, Lady Lethbridge." Belatedly, she realized she'd left home without a maid, which was so far beyond the proper etiquette she shuddered to know what the countess thought of her.

"You are quite welcome." The older woman settled into a low sofa while the viscount took the chair next to Cecilia's. "My son Lewis told me a couple of days ago that he'd entered into a courtship with you, so I had the thought that you and I should come to know each other better."

"It sounds logical, of course." She frowned as she bounced her notice between the two of them. "Will Lord Lethbridge join us for tea, then?"

"Unfortunately, he will not," the countess said with a quick shake of her head. "He is currently meeting with his man-of-affairs for a few things."

Beside her, the viscount snorted. "And he doesn't know Mama issued you the invitation to tea," he said, with a rather cheeky grin. "When he is informed of it after the fact, I'm sure he will be *quite* vocal in his displeasure."

"Hush, Alexander, else you will frighten our guest away," the older woman said, with a faint frown. "And we wouldn't want that."

Cecilia tamped down the urge to heave a sigh. It was difficult to determine why the countess had invited her today. "Why will the earl prove upset? Did he not want me to come here today or even meet with his mother?" Did she sound as insecure as she felt?

"Calm yourself, Miss Dawson." Compassion reflected in the viscount's eyes. "He will only be out of sorts because he hasn't seen you for two days. I would imagine the absence is grating on his nerves, but obligations have kept him from calling on you. Still, make no mistake. He mentions you quite often."

"I don't know if that's a good thing or a bad thing." Yet she took the words at face value. Glad for the reassurance, Cecilia nodded. "Thank you for the clarification."

Nothing else was said, for a footman brought in a tea service on a silver tray, which he set on the low table in front of the countess. Once he exited the room, the older woman was the first to break the silence.

"My son tells me that you are taking boxing lessons from him. Is that true?" As she spoke, the countess poured tea into a dainty bone china cup decorated with a tiny spray of painted flowers on the front.

"Um, yes, it is." If her nerves pulled any tighter, they would likely snap beneath her skin. After accepting the cup from her, Cecilia rushed to fill the silence. "I was quite desperate to visit the boxing salon."

"Why was that? Did you have designs on one of my sons?" Though it was said in a perfectly pleasant voice, the countess' eyes had narrowed slightly.

"Bad form, Mama," Lord Wexley hissed. "Behave." Once he'd accepted his own cup, he nodded at Cecilia. "Please continue, and don't mind my mother's overly protective probing."

"I did not, in fact." Still wishing to make a good impression on the woman, Cecilia offered a smile she hoped would disarm the countess. "I do accounting work at my father's shipping office, which is on the East India Dock. Sometimes this means that I am accosted and faced with unwanted and unwelcome attention from some of the works over there."

"Your father is not always at his office?"

"No. Sometimes he meets with clients and prospective investors while other times he must examine cargo that has come in." She paused to take a sip of tea, and though she wished she'd added a lump of sugar to the brew, she wasn't about to put forth a distraction from the conversation or have this woman potentially judge her on the size of the sugar lump. "In the past month, a Mr. Derrickson has been particularly vexing in his attentions that grow increasingly bold and violent. Instead of waiting around to become a victim, I brought myself to the boxing salon in a bid to request lessons in how I might defend myself."

Shock went through Lord Wexley's expression. Had he not known the reason for her willingness to learning fisticuffs, or did something else surprise him?

"That is quite a scandalous risk you took, Miss Dawson."

"Perhaps, but the alternative is even more unpleasant, wouldn't you say, Lady Lethbridge?" Refusing to back down, Cecilia continued, and took comfort from the warm tea in the porcelain teacup. "You might think it scandalous to come into a boxing salon that is a male domain, but I was desperate to keep myself alive. When I applied to your son and asked for lessons, I came in the disguise of a young man. No one there knew I was a woman, and in the event you wondered, I have just cause to mistrust men's intentions."

"Why is that, dear?"

With a sigh and a quick glance at the viscount, who gave her an encouraging nod, Cecilia rested her gaze on the countess. "I was engaged years ago."

"Oh?" Surprise lined the older woman's face. "To whom?"

"A Mr. Ulstead. He was the son of a viscount, and the match had been arranged by my father, who used to be a friend of the man's." She shrugged, for it was ancient history by now, but she was quite mollified that Lewis hadn't blabbed her history to his family. "During our courtship, everything was lovely and felt very magical. However, after we'd been engaged for a handful of months, Mr. Ulstead began showing the true sense of who he was."

"Why did any of that bring you to my son's boxing salon?" Confusion sounded in the countess' voice. "What happened?"

"To put it bluntly, he beat me. He had quite the temper, and whenever anything displeased him, he took out that anger on me." She kept her gaze firmly glued to the cup and saucer in her lap. "Yes, it is highly embarrassing, and no doubt you'll say I should have kept that to myself for it is scandalous to admit, or even perhaps that it was my duty as an engaged woman." The lump of emotion in her throat caused her breath to catch, but after a swallow, she kept going. "Eventually, I couldn't bear it any longer and couldn't continue to hide the bruises or keep myself locked in the townhouse, so I told my father."

The viscount leaned forward in his chair as shock still ruled his expression. "Did he run the man off?"

"He did." She allowed a tiny smile. "Honestly, I thought the man was run out of England, for I hadn't seen him for years… until the other day when Lewis fought him in that bout. I had no idea Mr. Ulstead even knew how to box let alone had become a prize fighter."

Lady Lethbridge gasped. "You attended a bout?"

Before she could answer, Lord Wexley interrupted. "She went with us in disguise. There was no danger of her being seen."

"That is the height of scandal, Alexander!" Censure rang in

the countess' voice. "Have you all gone mad?"

He ignored her. "No wonder Lewis was adamant that he win the bout. Did you tell him who his opponent truly was?"

Slowly, Cecilia nodded. "Yes, but I told him days before how Mr. Ulstead had treated me." She took a sip of tea. "Perhaps I shouldn't have said anything to him, for it's not the best of subjects, but I believe in being honest, and if my words can either call attention to the plight of women or help others to understand…" Her words trailed off, for would it even matter with the countess?

For long moments, Lady Lethbridge remained silent. Finally, she sighed and looked at her son. "Did Lewis win the match?"

"Unfortunately, he did not due to being a bit distracted, I think, for it was clear Mr. Ulstead didn't have the same skill as Lewis."

"I see." Then she landed her attention on Cecilia. "You must have been frightened when you entered the boxing salon for the first time." It wasn't a question.

She nodded. "I was, but something had to change, and if I wanted that, it needed to start with me."

"I can't imagine how much fortitude it took on your part to make those first steps or to survive all that you have," the countess said in a soft voice. "You have my respect, Miss Dawson, even though doing any of that is the height of scandal."

"I can only be who I am, Your Ladyship, and how could I be happy with myself if I allowed such abuse and disrespect to continue?" In that moment, she didn't care if the countess approved of her or not. She was proud of the woman she was becoming.

"Well said, Miss Dawson," Lord Wexley said, with a nod and amusement dancing in his hazel eyes so like Lewis'. "I can see why Lewis wished to court you."

"Thank you. He is no slouch in overcoming disappointments and obstacles himself." In silence, she finished her tea. Though she might want a couple of the honey cakes resting on the tray, she refrained from asking, for her appetite had fled. Oddly, she had missed Lewis over the past two days, and that was something that had never happened to her when it came to men.

"Thank you for coming, Miss Dawson," Lady Lethbridge said. The emotions in her eyes were inscrutable, but her tone was clearly dismissive. "While you are a lovely woman and you have more mettle in your little finger than most people I have met, I'm certain you will understand when I say that you aren't what I have envisioned for my oldest son. Far too scandalous, and that will bring gossip and rumors to the Stapleton name. Lord knows we don't need any more of that."

Both she and Lord Wexley gasped.

"Mama, for shame!" he hissed in outrage. "Who the devil cares if she's not of the *beau monde* or even an heiress?"

"What?" Stunned, Cecilia gaped at the woman. "With all due respect, Lady Lethbridge, but I don't believe any of this is your decision. Unless I hear the same from Lewis, you will need to keep your opinions to yourself." Her hand shook so badly, she was obliged to set her cup and saucer on the table, then she stood. Then, to her horror, tears welled in her eyes, and slight panic rose in her chest.

"Do you know who you are talking to, Miss Dawson?" Shock threaded through the countess' voice and lay stamped over her face.

"I do, sadly, and I thought you might have been more well-rounded since you've raised three boys into upstanding adults, and you've kept your family together after being made a widow in trying circumstances." As quickly as she could, Cecilia scrambled to her feet. Her cheeks were hot with outrage. "Regardless, I'm sorry you are basing your acceptance on criteria many women can never fill, but I should hope that seeing your son calm and perhaps content would make a difference."

Lord Wexley shot into a standing position. "Please don't go, Miss Dawson. My mother isn't usually so rude."

"That very well may be so, but worry for her son or her family shouldn't be made an excuse to treat someone else badly." She gave him a small grin. "Thank you for *your* kindness." Then she glanced at the countess. "Thank you for the invitation and the tea. Please have Lewis call on me as soon as he can."

From the press of her lips into a tight line, Cecilia rather doubted that she would convey the message to her son.

With a half-stifled sob, she fled the room.

Though Lord Wexley called after her, she ignored him and ran toward the stairs. As the first drop of moisture fell to her cheek, she rushed down the stairs like a madwoman, barely waited for the footman to open the door for her. Then she continued to run along the pavement, for the distance between the Marylebone neighborhood and Manchester Square where she lived was quite short.

What would she do now? Despite her words of bravery not two minutes past, if Lewis' mother didn't approve of her, how could he defy the countess and continue to see her socially or any other way? She ignored, too, the suspicious ache in her heart that indicated she might care for the earl far more than she should.

Such a stupid ninny you are, Ceci, to fall for a man who is quite unattainable.

Chapter Fourteen

July 2, 1817
Stapleton Boxing Salon
Mayfair, London

OVER AND OVER again, Lewis drilled his fists into one of the sandbags, wouldn't let up even when his left shoulder throbbed, and his knuckles turned red.

He'd retreated to the salon after having dinner with Alexander at the club as a way to clear his thoughts and work out some of his anger so he wouldn't say something he would regret. An hour before dinner, Alex had told him that their mother had summoned Lia to tea yesterday and then subsequently rejected her, which had caused her to run out of the house in tears.

Surprise hadn't been the biggest emotion he'd experienced at the time, but anger had certainly been up there. He'd taken his mother to task, and though she'd also broken down into tears, she'd said she'd only been trying to protect him. Oddly enough, the overwhelming feeling guiding him right now was confusion, perhaps disappointment, and...

And what, Lewis? What are you not admitting to yourself?

Another few punches landed into the bag before he resumed his previous thought process.

As shocking as it would sound to other people—even to himself—he cared for Cecilia in all the ways that mattered. In fact, he would go so far as to say that he might be falling in love with her. Hell, he wanted to be everywhere she was, wished to know everything about her, looked forward to seeing her and hearing her counsel, even felt more calm when she was near. Because of her, he'd begun seeing life in a different way, and that in itself was a shock, for he'd thought being reared as an earl's son and being handed heavy responsibility was his only lot.

Not any longer.

She had opened a wealth of new opportunities for him, and he couldn't wait to explore them—with her. Could he be the earl he needed to be if he didn't have the right woman by his side? *Was* she the right one? He rather suspected she might be, but if his mother didn't approve and he went forward with his intentions to court Cecilia, would that put a rift into the family?

God, everything was too muddled to try and puzzle out, so he gave the sandbag another few punches.

To say nothing of that fear that after the disastrous tea with his mother, would he be able to convince Cecilia to spend time in his company again?

There was always hope, and after he completed his exercise, he planned to drive to her townhouse and call upon her despite the lateness of the hour. Perhaps her father would take pity upon him and invite him in at the very least to share a drink.

And then there was the bout he would enter into tomorrow night. It would get him out of the hell where he'd be expected to meet and dance with the eligible women he suspected his mother had invited. But on the other hand, he had doubts that his shoulder would hold, yet it had to.

Because he would give Mr. Derrickson the beating of his life for daring to molest Cecilia, yet when she discovered that was who he'd fight, would she ring a peal over his head?

He couldn't help his grin as he continued to drill his fists into the sandbag. No doubt she would, but then, he enjoyed it when she rebuked him; it meant someone cared about him beyond his family, and there was a certain satisfaction and a giddy sort of happiness in that.

"Lewis."

The echo of his name in *her* voice had him swinging about to glance at the door, and it wasn't his imagination. Truly, she stood there, clad in her useless disguise as a young man, and in the dim illumination from the single candle he'd lit over an hour ago, she was easily the most beautiful woman he'd even seen, even if she didn't look it just now.

"What are you doing here?" He grabbed up a towel from the floor and wiped the sweat from his face and neck.

"I haven't seen you for two days," she said in a low voice as she crept through the shadow-filled salon. "After I waited for word from you and not having it, I grew concerned about you, so I decided to come seek you out."

He admired her initiative, even as her worry for him tightened his chest and put gratitude and, dare he say, love into his throat. "How did you know to come here?"

"Where else would you be? When your mind is conflicted, you turn to boxing." Said as a matter of fact, even he could follow the logic.

"You know that about me after only knowing me for less than two weeks?" He wiped down his chest, then tossed away the towel.

"Yes." She nodded and then removed the slouch-style cap, resting it on a straight-backed wooden chair near the wall. "I have found when one has been bullied and beaten, one tends to observe things more than the usual person." Slowly, she approached him, unbuttoning her tweed jacket as she went. "I suppose you heard about my tea with your mother?"

"I did. Alexander told me not two hours past." His gaze hungrily roved over her form when she removed the jacket and draped it over the chair's back. "I'm sorry she said those things to you. She had no right."

Cecilia frowned. "No, she had every right; she is your mother. She no doubt wants what is best for you."

He snorted. "She is flirting with rudeness." Watching her, he moved to the shelf where the candle rested in a brass holder. Easily, he snuffed it out, and as the acrid scent of burning wick filled the air, the ghost of the smoke vanished into the shadows. "What if what she wants is *not* what I want?" he managed in a barely audible whisper while coming back to her location.

"That is your prerogative and privilege, of course, but I came here tonight to tell you goodbye." A mist of tears rose into her eyes. "I will not have it said that I broke up a family or led an earl astray, but neither can I occupy the periphery of your life and bear witness to you choosing a woman who might be equal to you in class, but all too wrong for you in every other way."

If her voice hadn't caught, if her chin hadn't trembled, if a sheen of tears hadn't filled her eyes, he would have been fine. But all of that *did* happen, and he crumbled, for he was only so strong, and he suddenly knew beyond all doubt that the best for him was her.

"Damn it, Lia, don't do anything rash." Then she was in his arms, and he tipped her head back to better avail himself of her lips.

For the space of a heartbeat, she paused, her gaze searching his, and before he could draw another breath, she lifted onto her toes, looped her arms about his shoulders, and kissed him back. Shortly thereafter, Lewis was lost. He chased the feeling of homecoming she gave him, for it was as if he'd never been welcomed as he was with her.

He slid his hands down her sides, then caught them beneath her thighs, easily lifting her up, and using the wall as leverage, he continued to plunder her mouth as if she would be imminently snatched from him.

To her credit, Cecilia wrapped her legs around his waist and held him all the tighter while fencing with his tongue. When she furrowed her fingers into the hair at his nape and she clung to him as if she feared this was their last time together, he uttered a soft growl.

Damn, he wanted her all too much—for everything—but for now, he would settle for claiming her body. "I don't know what I did right in my life to have you here with me now, but I'm bloody grateful for it." After all, he was merely an earl with a nearly empty title, and a busted-up body from his previous bouts in the boxing ring.

"Perhaps you shouldn't question fate," she whispered, and when he released her only to grasp her hand, she followed him into the office. "There is no understandable reason for us to be together, or what is between us—"

"No, I can't fathom we were thrown together for a fleeting moment." He was coming to rely on her far too much for that. "Lia, I…" How could he utter the words that hovered on the tip of his tongue when he didn't truly understand what it was he felt right now?

"Don't ruin the moment by saying something you don't mean or can't possibly fulfil." Yet the gleam in her eye arrested the wild beating of his heart for a few seconds, and he welcomed that pause, for being near her, wanting her as if she were vital to his very life, was quite overwhelming as well as exhilarating.

"How do you know I can't… or won't?"

"The odds are against us," she said in a soft whisper, and looked all the more lovely in the dark, for the Venetian blinds were in place on all the windows.

"I never contemplate the odds."

"It is one of the many things I admire about you." Then she closed the distance between them, put a hand on his shoulder and gently guided him close until he bent his head to hers. "Do you know why I adore sparring with you?"

"I couldn't begin to answer that with any authority. Everything you've done surprises me." At least that was the truth. He'd seen her confidence and bearing grow since their first meeting, and he couldn't be more proud of that.

"Knowing that I am growing my power, feeling the purchase of my fists into your mittens makes me feel wanton and uninhibited," she whispered and dropped her gaze to his mouth. "I never wish to knock you out, but I always hope you see me differently after every bout, that I make an impression on you."

Oh, dear God.

A rush of hot sensation moved through his shaft, hardening it. "You have indeed made quite the impression on me, and I would be an absolute nodcock not to take notice of you." His lips brushed hers. There was no doubt in his mind that he'd gone mad.

I am quite certain that I love her.

"Quite." With the veriest bit of pressure, she encouraged him even closer. Was she echoing his unspoken thought? Yes, complete and utter madness was what he felt. And it was somehow freeing. "What should we do about that?"

"I wonder…" He wanted her in a way that made absolutely no sense to the logical mind. Certainly, there were risks associated with all of it, yet… For the first time in his adult life, Lewis tossed caution to the winds. It was time to begin living his life as if he actually guided it, instead of letting responsibility prod him. Before he could think about ramifications or consequences, he slid his arms around her. "We are in luck, for I can think of a few things." And then he crushed his mouth to hers.

The attraction between them caught fire and pulled them into its vortex as he kissed her thoroughly and quite relentlessly. Her lips were soft but insistent, and she gave him back everything he offered. All too soon tongues were entwined, and hands glided over bodies. Shortly after, he had the buttons of her vest undone.

Cecilia wrenched away. "Regardless of what will happen in the future, I want you right in this moment." She followed the statement by kissing him with the verve and enthusiasm she showed to every aspect of her life… at least when it came to boxing.

What sort of gentleman would he be if he didn't oblige her?

Various bits of clothing fell to the floor: her vest and gloves, her sloppily tied cravat as well as her ill-fitting boots. Then he pulled Cecilia's shirt from her body, and he almost shot his wad in that moment, for tonight she wore stays beneath the shirt, and damn if that wasn't the most erotic thing he'd ever seen.

"Dear God, Lia, you're—"

She cut his words off with a fierce kiss. "No talking. If this is to be the last time I'm with you, I only want you." When she dropped to the mattress tick and beckoned to him in the dark and shadows, Lewis was lost.

"Damn." Quickly, he tugged off his boots. They fell to the floor with two resounding thuds. He kneeled before her and worked to pull off the breeches that had tempted him beyond reason since the first moment he'd met her. She manipulated the laces of her stays. Seconds later, she was gloriously naked with her body bared to his inspection, and the darling girl leaned back onto her elbows to let him look his fill.

This is so much better than our first time.

She was right. There was no need for words. He would show her his admiration instead—his love, if he were honest. With his gaze holding hers, he removed his breeches, uncaring that his member was proudly rampant to the point of pain, and when he came over her body, settling between her bent knees, a sigh escaped when he found her lips again with his.

If he weren't already fully besotted with her, kissing her, exploring her body as she did to him would have done the trick. Soft, silky skin met his wandering fingers, glided beneath his lips as he sought to re-familiarize himself with every nuance of her form. The slopes of her breasts, the curve of her hips, the gentle swell of her stomach all called to him, for his touch, and she was as lush and gorgeous as he remembered.

How could any man reject such a woman due to those curves, or perhaps a bit of extra weight, in favor of someone more in style?

Dear God, but she is a goddess!

The moment he closed his mouth on a pebbled pink nipple, she moaned and arched her back while he kneaded her other breast. The scent of violets teased his nose, and he couldn't have enough—of her, of her perfume, of the thought of them together to meet all the challenges life would throw at them. Lewis nuzzled the crook of her shoulder, nipped and nibbled a path between her breasts, over them, explored her navel while he pleasured her with his fingers.

Suddenly, this act was more than a simple bedding. It was worshipping this woman, telling her without words how much he adored and appreciated her, how much he wanted her in all the ways that mattered.

With a laugh that felt this side of wicked, he dipped his head between her splayed thighs and drew his tongue along her folds. Apparently, she hadn't expected that, for she gasped and squirmed from his attention. Chuckling against her skin, he encouraged that tiny bud at her center out of hiding and then set to work worrying it with his lips, alternately sucking it into his mouth and soothing it with swipes of his tongue. Cecilia held his head tightly against her flesh. In the next second she attempted to shove him away, but he could be stubborn when he wished.

Even in this they were well matched, and in this moment, he wouldn't stop until he'd sent her over the edge.

"Oh, oh. Oh!" A keening cry left Cecilia's throat the second he increased the friction against that nubbin. She squirmed, thrashed her head on the mattress tick. A red flush faintly stained her chest and cheeks in the dim illumination as she curled the fingers of one hand into his hair.

"It sounds as if you are in great need, Lia. Shall I send you over again?" Pure masculine smugness welled within him at the thought as he came back up her body.

"I didn't know it was possible. Wondered about it, of course, but had never experienced anything like that..."

Lewis cut off her words with a kiss he hoped knocked all thought from her mind. With an arm beneath one of her knees, he fit his tip to her opening, and when she nodded, he thrust his hips, penetrating her fully and as deeply as he could go.

"Dear God, Lewis..." She hooked her other leg around his, her heel snug against his arse. "You feel so lovely. I adore this moment, when you've joined with me and we are one." Cecilia's eyes popped open, and she trained them on his face. "As if I'm wanted simply for me."

He grunted. "You are. So much." Had he said too much? The fact he was nearly too far gone wasn't lost on him, for when it came to this woman, everything was more intense, carried greater impact and reward. Stroking into her beautiful, receptive body didn't make him feel as if he were a failure or if he had that terrible weight about his shoulders. All of that fell away as pleasure swelled and love for her took hold.

How was any of this possible with this one woman?

Over and over, he pumped until he found a rhythm and she matched it. One of her hands curled around his upper arm while the other she'd flung above her head to brace herself against the wall. It was just as well, for each consecutive thrust grew more powerful than the last, scooting her body over the mattress tick. All too soon, he was lost to the tight heat of her, floating on the snatches of moans and the soft sounds of encouragement she made at the back of her throat. Would that he could hear them for the rest of his life, to have this woman by his side for as long as he was alive.

"Lewis..."

"Hmm?" His eyes were half-shuttered, but hers were open and watching him, the irises darkened to sapphire.

"Give me all of you. Don't hold back." A waver of uncertainty had entered her voice. "For tonight..." She squeezed his arm and the slight pressure of her heel at his arse told him all he needed to know.

Does she feel the same for me?

He unexpectedly lost another piece of his heart to her in that moment. But he rose to the challenge and thrust again. Harder. Faster. Deeper. Claiming her now but laying down an unspoken promise for the future. Basically marking her as his. Showing her how much he adored her and appreciated her in his life.

All in an effort to pleasure this wonderful woman who'd sent his life tip over tail in a handful of days. It was all too much too fast, and his body had been primed for too long thinking about her basically non-stop since the first time he'd joined with her. Hot sensation rushed through his shaft, tingled in his stones as they drew tight to his body. Sweat trickled down his spine and at his temples, and still he worked her over, for he didn't want this coupling to end.

It did, as all things do, but in spectacular fashion. Cecilia's body stiffened. Her moans grew more intense, and as she slipped a hand between their bodies to touch the button he'd tormented earlier, he lost the remainder of his control. Never had he seen anything as titillating as a woman who knew exactly what she wanted, even during intercourse, especially from a woman like her who'd been previously abused and beaten, a woman who'd found her power and her voice simply from asking him to teach her how to box.

His release welled up and over him before he was ready. Lewis didn't just fall over the edge into bliss. Oh, no, not with Cecilia. He was hurtled, thrown, violently pitched into a whirling vortex of need and want as sparkling colors swirled around him, fighting to steal his breath and sap his strength. And he gave himself up to it in that moment, for this was exactly what it had felt like since Lia had entered his life.

A long scream of satisfaction came from her, ringing in his ears. She clutched at him in a bid to hold him close, her body shaking and her feminine walls convulsing around his shaft. He shivered both in exhaustion and awe while his length pulsed, and still he ground himself against her to prolong the sensations for them both.

Eventually, his strength gave out and he collapsed on top of her, his breathing as ragged as hers. Cecilia's arms came around him. She kissed his shoulder, his temple, his cheek, before pressing her trembling lips into the curve of his neck. Wetness came away on his skin.

Was she crying? "Are you well? Did I do something wrong, hurt you?" Emotion thickened his voice. "If so, I didn't mean to—"

"No, nothing like that. I'm…" A sound that was a cross between a sob and a laugh escaped her. "I just realized that I'm happy for the first time in a very long while indeed, and the fact that it is because of you is overwhelming."

"I know exactly what you mean."

For a long time, they remained like that, lost, sated, adrift on a sea of heated contentment and lethargy, and finally Lewis acknowledged to himself what he must have known at the back of his mind all along: he was indeed in love with this woman, and there was nothing to stop the slide. Even more startling, he didn't want to, damn his mother's eyes. She could either support his decision or he would walk out of her life, but he refused to go forward without Cecilia.

After the bout, once he came out the victor and put her attacker in his place, he would ask her to marry him.

And then finally, finally, he could go about the business of being happy himself.

Chapter Fifteen

July 3, 1817
No. 12 Balsam Court
Manchester Square
Mayfair, London

"OH, I'M SO nervous," Cecilia admitted to her father as she peered at herself in the cheval glass of her room.

The sound of her father's indulgent chuckle as he watched her from his spot on the trunk at the foot of her bed worked to calm her nerves a bit. "You have been out in society before, Ceci. I can't imagine that this ball would discomfit you so."

"But it does, for this ball is being thrown by the Countess of Lethbridge, and since I already had tea with her which didn't end well, I can't imagine what my reception will be." Despite that fact, excitement zipped up and down her spine. Though her father was a gentleman as well as an ex-naval captain and a merchant, and she had been in society to an extent, she had never been invited to anything thrown by someone so high on the instep such as the earl.

And this felt quite significant.

After they'd coupled last night, she and Lewis had lain together in the darkness and quiet. Every once in a while, they would talk about whatever struck their fancy, and just when she'd finished dressing to return home, he'd waylaid her, implored her with words and kisses to attend the ball with him tonight. Even though he'd said it didn't matter what his mother thought, *he* wanted her with him, and that was enough.

And oh, how much she wanted to believe him!

"I suspect the countess will change her mind once she sees how devoted her son is to you," her father said, with an eyebrow raised in challenge.

"Is he, then? Devoted to me?" It had been far too dark last night to read the emotions in his eyes as they'd explored each other, but if she were honest with herself, she'd felt that change in how he'd touched her, how he'd kissed her, in the tone of his voice.

"Don't be coy, my girl. I have seen far too many men in love—I've even been one when I met your mother—so I know a bit of what I speak."

"Oh, Papa, every time I think about the earl, I'm rendered so confused." She turned this way and that as she gazed into the cheval glass. "Is this gown fancy enough?"

When Lewis had first asked her to the ball, she'd gone through her clothing like a madwoman searching for a gown that might pass muster. Eventually, her father had taken pity on her, and they'd gone through the shops in Mayfair. Fortune and fate must have played a part, for at a modiste's shop, they came upon a gown already finished. The original customer decided at the last moment she didn't like the looks of the creation, so the modiste sold it to Cecilia's father at a discounted rate with minimal alterations to fit her form.

"You are a vision, Ceci. Any man would be lucky to have you on his arm."

"Ha. Thank you. I rather think you might cause a sensation with older ladies and widows, for you are quite dashing in your evening clothes." She smiled at her reflection, for the gown of steel blue silk brought out the deeper blues in her eyes, and with every movement, the hundreds of tiny crystal beads that lined the low bodice as well as the hem sparkled and twinkled. "I think you are quite biased." But in this gown, she didn't seem nearly as plump or short if that was believable.

"Perhaps I am."

"You should find a lady and marry again. Don't you think it time, Papa?"

"I am steadily coming 'round to the idea, especially because I'll wager you'll soon move into your own life."

She huffed even as heat seeped into her cheeks. "Do stop. Nothing is certain." When she'd left the boxing salon—Lewis insisted on summoning his carriage and escorting her home— he'd not spoken of a future, his or theirs combined.

"Hmm, I wonder." He adjusted the knot of his cravat, for he would attend the ball with her, and for that she was quite grateful. "So now that I've set your fears to rest regarding your attire and why you should be there, as well as discussing the possibility of me moving into the next phase of my life, why are you still nervous?"

"This night feels like an audition of sorts, even though I have already been rejected by the earl's mother, yet I retain doubts that anything will come of my friendship with Lethbridge."

"Ah." For long moments, he remained silent. "Are you certain what you share with the earl is simply a friendship?" When she didn't answer, her father continued. "You have already told me that you are taking boxing lessons at least twice a week. However, there have been other outings with the man."

She nodded. "I also told you he wished to pay his addresses to me." None of this had been a secret.

"Yes, this is so, but after those outings, when you came home, you are more happy than I've seen you in years. Why is that, I wonder?" There was no judgment in his expression, merely curiosity or perhaps speculation.

"Being with the earl, both during boxing lessons as well as being in a courtship with him, has been… eye opening. It is quite different from my last relationship." For he well knew what sort of a man Mr. Ulstead had been. "And it has been rather lovely having a man defend me from Mr. Derrickson while at your office."

He snorted. "I have done that as well, but I suppose that isn't as thrilling as having a big, strong hero do the same, a man who you can reward with kisses, hmm?"

Heat seeped into her cheeks once more. "There is that part of it, true. I am flattered about his attention, of course, but this ball seems to be the next step."

"Of course it is, Ceci. He wants you in his life formally."

"I don't know about that. There are far too many obstacles between us."

"None of that matters when love is involved." For long moments he regarded her. "*Are* you in love with Lethbridge? You've not known him for very long, but that doesn't matter either. Sometimes a person just has a feeling about someone else."

Did she love Lewis? "Oh, I don't know if that is how it is with me..." Yet after everything she had shared with him, after being ruined by him, after coupling with him, after loving him for everything he was and instead of everything he wasn't... As she glanced at her father, her eyes widened. "Oh dear, I *might* have fallen for him despite being wary of men in general."

"At least you have admitted it to yourself." His grin was soft, but amusement danced in his eyes. "Why do you feel this way? What makes the Earl of Lethbridge better than any of the men who have shown interest in you over the years? The ones you have ignored or kept yourself aloof from?"

"Lewis is... different. I can't explain it any better than that." She pressed her lips together as she attached blue topaz earbobs to her lobes. "He treats me with respect and admiration. He is proud of me during our boxing lessons and doesn't hesitate to tell me so." Then she slipped on opera-length ivory gloves. "When he looks at me, I have the feeling that he sees something in me beyond my body, and wants me for much more than the fleeting physical release." Tears welled in her eyes. "Beyond that, he has never laid a hand on me in anger or violence. That is quite astonishing, at least to me, and it frightens me a bit to know that is how women should be treated…"

"Because you are constantly looking for fault in him and wondering when he'll show you his true self," he finished for her in a soft voice.

"Yes, that is it exactly." Tears again welled in her eyes, and at least one of them escaped to her cheek. "Is it naïve of me to think he is only trying to win me before doing that? Or can I take a chance and trust that he is fully the gentleman that he claims?"

"No, my girl. You are anything but naïve, and you have every right to be wary. However, I believe you when you say he is different. You would have known deep down if he wasn't, and would never have allowed the relationship to progress so far." He stood, crossed the floor, and then wrapped his arms around her in a hug. "I hope for your sake he feels the same about you, but then, I am not worried about that."

"Why?" There was a certain comfort in that embrace, just like she remembered from her childhood years.

"Because any man who has heard the stories of your past, who has gone up against your willfulness, who has consented to enter into risk gossip and rumor enough to teach you how to box has interest in you beyond the shallow." When he pulled away, he grinned down at her. "I shall expect him to pay me a visit rather more sooner than later, for unless I miss my guess, he's charmed his way into scandal with you?"

Oh, dear heavens.

"Um… yes." The heat of embarrassment fired in her cheeks. "That is to say, he and I have enjoyed… There were a couple of times when we—"

"Stop, dearest. You needn't explain further for me." Though he grinned, concern reflected in his eyes. "If the earl isn't the honorable man you think he is, and if certain consequences arise due to your… being with him in such a way, I am fully prepared to move our family out of London and to somewhere in the country where you can escape the gossip."

"I appreciate your support." Another few tears fell, and she was afraid of her eyes being red rimmed by the time they arrived at the ball. "Only time will tell in that regard, so there is no point in talking about it right now." When the long-case clock in the corridor on the floor below chimed the nine o'clock hour, she sighed. "If we don't leave, we will be late."

"Very well." He nodded. "But if I have an opportunity to talk with Lord Lethbridge tonight, I *will* ask his intentions toward you. I will support you in any decision you choose to make, however, if he is merely toying with you—"

"I truly don't think he is, Papa," Cecilia said before he could utter his threat. "Unfortunately, everything is complicated, and *I* intend to enjoy myself tonight. Who knows when the next time I'll be asked to a ball will be."

Chapter Sixteen

Stapleton House
Marylebone, Mayfair
London, England

T HE TOWNHOUSE OWNED by the Stapleton family was quite large, a fact that had escaped Cecilia's notice when she'd come for tea, but then, she supposed an earl would need a relatively bigger space to entertain properly.

That being said, one of the reasons the dwelling *was* so large was to contain a ballroom, and the moment her father escorted her into the space, her jaw dropped open. No, she wasn't a stranger to attending society functions, but the room was decorated with a caring hand and by someone with an eye to details.

Large vases filled with riots of long-stemmed flowers as well as wildflowers and other greenery rested in all four corners on pedestals that resembled Grecian columns. Other, smaller vases and urns were also filled with flowers and set in strategic places about the room. Swags made with greenery, palm fronds, and flowers had been tacked above the windows and double doors, as well as the French-paned doors that led into the rear gardens which then rolled directly into a square beyond the property. The parquet floor of the dance space gleamed, and had been polished into a high shine that reflected the flicker and glow of the candles in the crystal chandelier that hung above it. Wall sconces provided additional illumination that, coupled with the flash and glitter from the gemstones in the women's jewelry, made the room into a magical place.

"This is beautiful," Cecilia said in a hushed voice, as she continued to take in all the decorations. "And look how the colors in the gowns contrast so greatly with the black of the men's evening suits." It was perfection. "I wish I knew how to paint."

Her father patted her gloved hand that rested on his arm. "There are other ways to remember this night, my girl." When he glanced about the room, he grinned. "Look, there is the earl. He is leading his mother out for the opening set." Then he put his lips near her ear. "While I admit he is quite a fine specimen, his mother doesn't resemble the dragon you've described."

"Papa!" But she snorted. "I never said that she was." As she spoke, Cecilia watched the pair as they were joined by a handful of other couples for the first country reel of the evening. Yes, the countess was lovely in a gold satin gown paired with emerald jewelry, but the whole of her attention rested on Lewis. "He is so handsome tonight," she whispered to her father.

Clad in the requisite dark evening clothes, he was every inch the earl tonight with his light brown hair tamed and styled with the help of a touch of pomade. A sapphire stick pin winked from the starched folds of his cravat and a matching blue spark of fire came from a gemstone on the signet ring on his right pinky finger. Though fading bruises still decorated various portions of his face, he was still the most beautiful man she'd seen of late, with the breadth of his shoulders showed to perfection by the black tailcoat and the length of his legs giving her flights of fancy.

"Ah, Ceci, I'd say you are quite tip over tail for the man," he said in a low voice, with amusement threading through it. "It is my fondest wish that this night will bring you everything you hope it will."

For the first time in her life, she cautiously let herself look forward to the future. "So do I." While she followed Lewis with her gaze, the music from a string quartet filled the air, and it was a lovely start to the evening.

Eventually, her father left her side, for he had discovered that a few of his friends were in attendance, so he happily took himself off to one of the card rooms.

She wasn't left alone for long on the sidelines, for Lewis soon came looking for her once his duties to the party guests had been fulfilled. "You are quite handsome tonight, Your Lordship," she said in a low voice, as he joined her at the side of the room.

"Such gammon, Miss Dawson," he said, with a twinkle in his eye as he stuck to formality. "I have seen my visage in a looking glass; the bruises aren't exactly an enhancement."

"Badges of honor."

"Perhaps." When he gave her that special grin he seemed to set aside exclusively for her, flutters chased through her lower belly. Then he offered her a gloved hand. "While I'm glad you decided to come tonight, I rather wish we were alone." He dropped his voice to a whisper. "However, for the moment, will you share this next dance with me? It's a Viennese waltz."

Despite her nerves that flared once more, Cecilia nodded. "I will." The moment she slipped her fingers into his palm, and he closed his hand around hers, a shiver of awareness went down her spine. "How is your mother tonight?" As of yet, she hadn't come into contact with the countess.

"She is happy being the center of attention, I think." As he led her to an open space on the dance floor, he chuckled. "However, I feel she is watching me like the proverbial hawk, for she has invited several eligible women tonight, and I know she hopes there will be a spark between me and one of them."

Worry prompted Cecilia to frown. "Has there been?"

He met her gaze with his, and his grin was both disarming and need-inspiring. "There is only one woman in this room for whom my blood burns." Before she could reply, he put his lips to the shell of her ear. "Didn't our time together last night show you the truth of my words?"

"Oh!" Heat sneaked into her cheeks, and then there was no time to say anything further, for the first notes of the waltz erupted into the air, and Lewis set them into motion.

Although she enjoyed the exercise that dancing provided, it was quite annoying to begin the set in Lewis' partnership but then transfer to another partner as the steps progressed. Each time they were apart, she followed him with her gaze, never truly remembering what her new partner said to her. And when she came back into his vicinity, so much happiness bubbled through her chest that she didn't know how to conduct herself.

"Would that I stood on the sidelines," he whispered, with an enigmatic grin.

"Why is that?" She could hardly breathe with him so close.

"You are quite graceful when you perform the steps of this waltz. I wish that I had the freedom to watch you, for at the end, your partner would need to bring you back to me."

Once more, the steps shifted and she was shuttled to a different partner, who she barely gave a smile to. Every second she was away from the earl seemed like an eternity, and when she was obliged to come back into his orbit, a shuddering sigh left her throat.

"If I didn't know better, Your Lordship, you are quite the romantic."

His chuckle sent eddies of awareness sailing over her skin. "Let us just say I remain hopeful." That grin of his grew wider. "I adore that shade of blue on you. It makes you seem quite mysterious and magical. Your eyes alone tonight would summon men to your side."

What a lovely thing to say. She lost another piece of her heart to him in that moment. It was time to make a bit of a confession to him. "There is only one man I wish to snare tonight."

Before he could offer a comment, the waltz came to an end. Then he offered her his arm, and as she laid her hand on his sleeve, he escorted her back to the side of the room.

"Thank you for sharing that waltz with me, Your Lordship."

He nodded. "If the musicians weren't having a bit of a break just now, I would claim the next set with you as well." Then he winked and her heart skipped a beat. "It would certainly send a message throughout the assemblage, wouldn't it?"

"A pity, that." She glanced about the room, and when her gaze collided with that of Lord Wexley's, Cecilia lifted a hand in greeting. He acknowledged her but frowned. Was he not enjoying himself tonight? "Perhaps we should take in a bit of air in the rear garden?" And perhaps he might try to steal a kiss.

The earl's expression fell. "While that would be lovely, I'm afraid I need to step away from the ball for a few hours."

"What? Why?"

He shook his head. "Duncan has promised to look after you and keep you entertained in my absence."

That made absolutely no sense. "Where are you going?"

"I can't tell you." And his gaze shifted to where Lord Wexley stood checking the time on his pocket watch.

Warning bells immediately clanged inside her head. Was this the horrible thing she'd been waiting for? "Tell me the truth. Do you have a mistress?"

"No. No!" He shook his head, and once more held her gaze with his. "This has nothing to do with a mistress or any other woman."

As people milled through the crowded ballroom and the sound of talking and laughter floated about her, Cecilia frowned at him as her chest grew tight. "Is this your way of saying you don't wish to be with me any longer, but that you're too much a coward to tell me?" Panic lodged a ball of tears in her throat. Had she been so wrong about him, then?

"Oh, Lia, of course not." With a hand on hers, he led her farther near the wall and out of foot traffic. "In fact, I rather think I care for you far too much."

When she peered into his face, nothing except the stark truth was reflected there. "How so?" If that was true, she wanted to hear it. Perhaps it would explain his bizarre announcement.

"I…" The earl blew out a breath. Then he nodded. "Truth be told, I'm leaving the ball with Alexander to enter into a bare-knuckle boxing match over the border of Hertfordshire County in Hertsmere. In fact, I'll be going against one of the men who accosted you at your father's shipping outfit."

Fear twisted down her spine in icy tendrils. "Who?"

"Mr. Derrickson."

"What?" If her outcry was a touch louder than she'd intended, she couldn't help it. "Are you a nodcock? He is quite the boxer in his own right, is always bragging about bouts that he's won and the purses he's taken. As if that would ever impress me while he was hurting me." She shook her head while tears sprang into her eyes. "You are going to be killed out there."

A frown took possession of his mouth, and all she wanted to do was kiss it away. "You don't think I can best him." It wasn't a question, and it had put his dander up.

"No, that's not it at all." She pressed her lips together as words flew through her mind. "In fact, I *know* you can win against him, but at what cost? Your shoulder is weak and your knee isn't stable." How did she make him understand that he had nothing to prove to anyone? Daring much, Cecilia laid a palm against his cheek even though they were in public. She held his gaze, searched it, perhaps in an effort to memorize every dear feature of his face. "I am not strong enough to lose you, Lewis." It was the best she could do as a confession, since they weren't alone.

For long moments, the earl remained silent. Then he slowly shook his head but kept hold of her free hand. "I must. For your honor, to make certain Mr. Derrickson will no longer bother you. To show him that he has no claim to you."

"While I appreciate that, I can take care of myself." She didn't want him to do this foolish thing and perhaps gain irreparable harm to himself.

"Yes, you can, but you shouldn't have to." He brought her hand to his lips and kissed the back. "Let me shoulder some of the burden."

Though her heart squeezed, she shook her head. "Why can't we do this together?"

"Bouts are illegal for men. It would be certain scandal for a woman. And I… I care too much for you to let that happen. I don't want the gossips to get hold of you if I can help it." He paused and a muscle in his cheek ticced. "There are things I would say to you after this bout is over…"

"Oh!" Did that mean he would ask for her hand? Though that was exciting enough, fear for his safety tamped down her reaction. "But I—"

"Please, Lia, I must go if I'm to make the bout in time and not forfeit the entry fee or my reputation as a boxer. Especially not to that bounder." He nodded at his middle brother, who was making his way across the dance floor toward them.

"Fine." She swallowed heavily but still wished to take refuge in tears. "Please be careful."

"I will. I promise." Then he released her hand.

"And Lewis?"

"Hmm?"

"I *do* believe in you, and I'm proud of you," she managed in a choked whisper. "Keep him on your right side, wrap your knee with cloth beneath your breeches to render it more stable, and you should be all right, and do remember that he sometimes favors his left wrist. I believe he broke it some time back when a shipping container slammed into it."

"Thank you." With a nod and a wealth of emotions in his eyes, he left the ballroom with Lord Wexley keeping pace beside him.

Why did it feel as if her whole world had abandoned her as he disappeared from sight. Before she could decide what to do with herself or at the very least wrangle her emotions under control, the countess joined her and immediately took her aside.

"Why are you upset, Miss Dawson?" she said, in lieu of a greeting.

It simply wouldn't do to show another vulgar display of

rudeness in front of this woman, especially in light of what Lewis would undertake soon. "I shouldn't say." In fact, she owed the countess an apology, but it sat wrong in her belly to take the high road when she'd done nothing wrong.

The countess laid a gloved hand on Cecilia's arm. Concern shadowed her eyes. "Did my son upset you? Did he end his courtship?"

Is that what she wanted to know? If so, why did she appear distressed about it? Tamping down hard on her annoyance, Cecilia shook her head. "It's not my secret to tell." She dashed at the escaped tears on her cheeks and wished the floor would open and swallow her whole.

Before their conversation could continue, Lewis' youngest brother joined them. She met Lord Frampton's gaze, where the same concern brewed that she struggled with.

He cleared his throat. "I believe Miss Dawson is annoyed and angry because Lewis is going to fight in a bout in about ninety minutes' time with a beast of a man."

"What?" The countess seemed far too flabbergasted for her reaction not to be genuine. "Why? He's not sufficiently recovered from his last fight." She huffed. "In fact, he's just not whole and should stop such nonsense anyway."

Some of Cecilia's control broke. "The earl *is* whole enough," she protested as she glared at the countess—her potential mother-in-law. "Yes, I was upset when he told me what he planned, and yes, he's doing it on some misguided sense of defending my honor, but that doesn't mean he shouldn't or can't. It was his decision."

For the space of a few heartbeats, both the countess and her youngest son stared at her. Finally, the countess nodded. "You don't think he should fight, either?"

"Of course not! I can defend myself, but he didn't listen to me because he's honorable."

A frown creased the countess' brow. "Then why is he going out at all? What did you promise him if he would win?"

Heated annoyance rose in her chest. "Nothing. There were no promises, and I asked him to leave it be, but he's quite stubborn." She crossed her arms beneath her breasts. "I have been bothered by the man he'll fight, but Lewis wishes to teach him a lesson despite my doubts. I can cold-cock that bastard he's fighting the same as he can. He tutored me well enough, and I *did* manage to land him on his arse once during lessons. So why he thinks he needs to do this as some point of honor is beyond me." As silence reigned, she realized she'd made all of that an audible outburst in response to a countess, and she gasped. "Good heavens. I am so sorry."

Lord Frampton gazed at her with admiration in his eyes. "Hear hear, Miss Dawson. Good show. Perhaps you are exactly what my bullheaded brother needs to keep him in line."

Heat slapped at her cheeks. "I don't think—"

Laughter from the countess interrupted her. She offered a disarming smile. "I am inclined to agree with Duncan. You must care for Lewis deeply if you're upset he's going to this fight."

"Oh, I…" What was there to say after that last outburst? "I don't want to see him hurt."

"It is quite all right, dear." In a shocking turn of events, the countess took Cecilia's hand and squeezed her fingers. "I love him too." Then a faint blush stained her cheeks. "I should probably offer you an apology for what I said to you at tea the other day. Now that I see how much you care for my son, I can admit I was wrong about you."

Cecilia's lower jaw fell open. "I appreciate that but—"

Lord Frampton chuckled. "You ladies can sort yourselves later. We should go after him and in the very least, make certain he knows he's supported."

"After who?" her father asked, as he approached their group.

Good heavens. Can this evening get any worse?

"My son, Lewis," the countess said. She then introduced herself. "I am the Countess of Lethbridge, and I have just been told my son intends to fight a brute of a man in an illegal bout tonight."

"Lovely to meet you, Your Ladyship." Her father's eyes sparkled. "I am Captain Dawson, Cecilia's father."

"A pleasure, Captain." The countess bestowed a smile on him.

"Well then, now that the pleasantries are out of the way…" He nodded. "I agree that we should all go after the earl, and once he's won the fight, we should collectively give him a dressing down and hope he'll give up this insanity if he wishes for a future."

The whole situation was becoming a farce. "This is getting out of hand," Cecilia murmured. "I'm going myself."

"No." Lord Frampton shook his head. "All of us will go or no one will." He met the eyes of each of them. "Lewis will need every bit of support he can have during the fight, and who better than the people who love him the most?"

Her father cleared his throat. "With all due respect, Your Ladyship, you shouldn't leave your own ball."

The countess laughed, and the tinkling sound blended with the other sounds buzzing through the ballroom. "Dear Captain Dawson, I am a widow and the mother of three grown sons." She grinned. "I have been through crazier things than this, and by rights, I can do what I want. The ball will either carry on without me or it won't. Either way, it's not the end of the world, but I refuse to let this night be the potential end to my firstborn son. He still has much to offer the world."

"As you can see, my mother is quite stubborn in her own right." Lord Frampton's grin was wide. "For myself, I'm going to see Lewis get his clock cleaned." At the protests from both Cecilia and his own mother, he put up a hand. "Mostly, but he *is* my brother, so if he doesn't win the bout, I'll go after his opponent personally. No one kicks the arse of a Stapleton."

"How has this grown out of hand?" she asked her father in a soft voice.

"When you have a collection of strong personalities, this is what happens." He merely chuckled. "I'm accompanying you there because someone must, and I believe the night won't simply end with a boxing match." He winked at her. "Shall we get on with it, then?"

None of that calmed the fear coiling coldly inside her belly. "I hope he comes out of this fight more intact than not." Because if he did, she would give him a proper dressing down for frightening her so badly. Did he not know how much she cared for him?

At least now she'd admitted it to herself. That was a huge step for her.

Chapter Seventeen

A meadow in Hertfordshire
Site of the illegal boxing match

I F CECILIA THOUGHT her nerves were strung too tight at the ball, that was nothing compared to the unease she felt now as she exited the closed carriage.

Since there had been no time to go home and retrieve the clothing she'd previously worn as a disguise, the countess had let her borrow a cloak, for that austere lady absolutely refused to leave the privacy of the vehicle. Cecilia had agreed with alacrity, for there was no way she would be confined or hidden away, not when Lewis' future might hang in the balance.

With the hood up and the frog fastenings secured, the garment went all the way to the ground, for the countess was a few inches taller than her, but she didn't care that the hem dragged through the grass. Her father walked on one side of her while Lord Frampton occupied her other side. As they approached the swelling crowd in the clearing, the urge to retch grew strong.

"There's quite a crowd," she murmured to her father, while keeping one eye on the ground to make certain she didn't step into horse excrement or a hole.

He nodded. "Boxing is a lucrative sport." With his gray greatcoat, beaver felt top hat, and black muffler, he was as nondescript as she in the black cloak with its hood in place.

"What is wrong with these men that they willfully pay hard-earned coin to watch other men beat each other, sometimes senseless? Why is this considered entertainment?"

It was her father who answered. "Since ancient times, people have thronged to the primal attraction of seeing one of their fellows beaten or killed. I have no idea why it inflames so many, or why that curiosity exists to see one of their own suffer." He shrugged as they pushed their way through the crowds. "Humanity is and always will be perverse and bloodthirsty, especially when in concentrated groups. This leads them into trouble at times."

Lord Frampton snorted. "Perhaps humans have never gotten over their cave-dweller instincts, and as long as it's not them being pummeled, it's acceptable." He glanced at her. "Be glad we don't live in the time of the gladiators; Lewis could be out there fighting lions or bears."

"You are all horrible," she hissed in a fierce whisper.

"Perhaps we are, but then, women still manage to love us anyway," her father jested back at her, to the amusement of the earl's brother. "And in truth, much of it happens because of the women we love."

"Do shut up," she bit off, not in the mood for frivolity when she was so worried about Lewis.

"I sometimes think you have more courage than any of us, Ceci," he replied, as they fought against the crush in the attempt to move closer to a roped off area which served as the boxing ring.

"It also takes a fair amount of courage to decline such a nod-cock invitation." If her response was a touch more waspish than she'd intended, so be it. "I will be certain to give Lewis a dressing down about this when this ridiculous bout ends."

Lord Frampton turned to her, temporarily halting her forward momentum. "He is doing this *for* you, Miss Dawson. You don't need to agree with it, but men like Lewis? They will defend the people they love until there is nothing left to give. Whether he's fighting for your honor, your protection, or to fill the family coffers, he will give it his all because he cares. At least show him the respect he deserves because there are precious few men who will do even that these days."

The censure in his voice humbled her. Then his words sank into her brain. *Lewis loves me?* "You're right." She nodded. "Thank you for the reminder, but just know I'm frightened for him."

The man nodded. "We all are. Now, let us discern his corner and go support him."

Further conversation proved near impossible with the sheer volume of shouts and calls from the spectators. To say nothing of last-minute wagers being made. By and large, men made up the gathering, though there were a few ladies present. She had her doubts as to whether they were part of the *ton*. Yet she couldn't help wondering if some women had chosen to come in disguise. Cecilia blocked most of the noise out, for her attention lay focused on the men inside the makeshift square. Lewis occupied one corner, along with Mr. Derrickson, as well as Lord Wexley, who stood talking to his brother, no doubt putting him in the proper mindset.

"Oh, my," she breathed, and shamelessly continued to stare.

Lewis had stripped to the waist, of course, for too many clothes restricted movement. Clad only in a pair of black silk evening breeches, every inch of his torso was on display. From a flat abdomen with defined muscles that still retained bruises from his last bout, to the spattering of brown hair on his chest, to the impressive width of his shoulders, he was a fine specimen of male perfection, and she well remembered how that honed body slid against hers in heat and passion.

He did a quick series of stretches that showed him to every advantage while she continued to gawk. Had his legs always been so taut and powerful? His backside so tight? Of course they had, but that didn't stop her from wanting to tug him away from what would surely be folly and have her wicked way with him. What had the man done to her that she would harbor such naughty

thoughts? *Dear God, I want to lick spilled champagne from that belly...*
Heat blazed in her cheeks, but she couldn't look away.

"He is certainly most impressive."

"Get hold of yourself, Miss Dawson," Lord Frampton whispered into her ear. "Though Lewis *is* the most fortunate of men if he can arouse your admiration." Amusement rang in his tone.

"Do shut up." But her admonishment sounded a trifle breathless and ineffectual. When Lewis scanned the crowd and his gaze met hers, a thrill lanced down her spine. It echoed in her core as a throb of desperate need. He flashed a grin but the emotions in his eyes were too difficult to read. Butterflies erupted in her belly. "Oh, my goodness, I think I'm in a spot of bother."

"You are just now realizing this?" Her father nudged her ribs with an elbow. "I'll wager the rest of us have seen that in you already."

There was nothing to say, for it was true. She'd fallen in love with the boxer, and she didn't quite know what to do about it. Then her gaze jogged to Mr. Derrickson, and since he'd been staring at her anyway, when their gazes collided, another round of cold fear twisted down her spine, especially as he narrowed his eyes.

Just as surely as she realized she loved Lewis quite desperately, she knew Mr. Derrickson wouldn't show compassion toward him during the fight. In fact, he would keep going until the earl was nearly dead.

A short, rotund man stepped into the roped off area. As he beckoned to both fighters, the roar of the crowd hushed. "Today's match is between Lewis Stapleton, the Earl of Lethbridge, and London's local favorite champion, Mr. Thomas Derrickson. No doubt this match will prove exciting with two such headline makers." The man beamed at the audience, which cheered and strained forward. "May the best man win." He then rang a brass handbell and slowly backed away from the combatants.

Another man she assumed was a doctor stood off to one side,

outside the ring, with two men who would serve as referees.

Lewis and Mr. Derrickson circled each other, their bare feet making no sound on the grassy clearing. Cecilia moved closer to the rope as she tried to keep her gaze on the earl. Then, Lewis made the first move with a brilliant punch to the man's left cheek. The bigger man dodged and darted away, but quickly spun and tagged him with a right hook that snapped Lewis head backward.

"Oh, no!" She held onto Lord Frampton's arm as tightly as he would allow.

"It's early in the round. Don't worry." The soothing tones did nothing to relieve her anxiety.

"How can I bear to watch the rest of the fight when I fear for this round?"

Her father patted her shoulder. "Hope for the best, my girl."

Over and over the boxers parried and punched, danced away, then came back with impressive form. The sound of flesh hitting flesh echoed in her ears, and each time Lewis received a hit, she gasped, but she couldn't help but admire the flow of his body and the power he held. Yes, she'd watched him fight before, but there was something different about this time, perhaps because she looked at him through a veil of newly realized feelings.

Mr. Derrickson charged Lewis with a shoulder into his chest, and as he attempted to regain his balance, the bigger man treated him to a solid punch to the chin that had Lewis landing hard on his back, gasping for breath.

"No!" Cecilia strained forward, but Lord Frampton grabbed onto her arm. "We have to help." Her heartbeat accelerated, racing through a horribly tight chest. "I have to go to him."

"We don't and we won't." A frown pulled down the corners of his lips. "This is a public boxing match where women are generally not welcome. Have some decorum. The last thing we want is for Lewis to feel embarrassed or prove distracted."

"Of course." She shook off the man's hold and pushed her way to the ropes as Lewis staggered to his corner. Lord Wexley sat with one knee outthrust for Lewis to perch upon.

"Damn it, Lewis, you must concentrate, or you'll lose in the next round." His brother lifted a ladle of water to the earl's lips in the absence of a water boy. "What the hell is wrong with you?"

"I'm trying." He pushed away the ladle after having a sip. "He is strong and has rage on his side."

"Then you need to summon yours," Lord Wexley said with a frown. "You usually put down an opponent with efficiency. We cannot afford another loss."

Dear heavens, this isn't the way to motivate him! Cecilia couldn't stand it any longer. "Lewis." When he glanced at her, pleasure lit his hazel eyes. "Please be careful. Focus and don't think about everything that is weighing you down."

"Fisticuffs aren't dangerous." He grinned. "I can manage."

She snorted in an effort to cover her concern. "Show me what you're made of and stop dawdling. I want you in one piece after this bout."

"I'll see what I can do. Such a managing baggage you've become." He winked, and heat invaded her cheeks.

The handbell rang again, signaling the start of the second round, so Lewis left his corner. Both Stapleton brothers stared at her.

"I'm concerned for the earl's safety."

Lord Wexley grinned as he looked her up and down. "You are quite bold Miss Dawson, and I applaud that, but there is scandal in the offing since you've come out here to watch a bout without a disguise."

She arched an eyebrow. "Yes, well, when your brother goes haring off to do something like the proper nodcock he is, someone with sense must come along to make sure he doesn't get himself killed."

Her father chuckled. "Don't get her dander up, Lord Frampton. She can prove rather tenacious."

Surprised laughter came from the viscount. "Damn. Does Lewis know the depth of your regard?"

Before she could answer, the handbell rang once more. Cecilia diverted her attention to the ring and frowned when she spied Mr. Derrickson on his back with Lewis grinning at the roaring crowd.

"Well, drat. You've made me miss his triumph." When she glanced at the earl, he winced as he rubbed his left shoulder.

"My apologies." Amusement threaded through Lord Wexley's rejoinder, but he exchanged a speaking glance with his brother. "To be fair, it is only the end of round two."

She released a sound of frustration. "Oh, you Stapleton boys are so aggravating at times!"

All three men chuckled at her outburst.

Why are men so annoying?

Round three began as soon as Mr. Derrickson gained his feet. Apparently neither fighter wished for a break.

The footwork, as well as darting and dodging, brought Mr. Derrickson closer to her location at the rope.

"I'll put down the fecking earl soon enough, and that means you'll belong to me by default."

She blew out a breath. "I am not an object to be owned, but regardless, Lethbridge *will* prevail."

"Not unless I end him permanently."

As fear played icy fingers down her spine, she glued her attention to the fight. Though Mr. Derrickson came back strong, Lewis held his ground. As each punch was exchanged, the roar of the crowd intensified. People strained forward around the roped off area. Some called out encouragement to their preferred boxer.

"Damn it, Lewis, it's step, step, upper cut and then a round-house kick," Lord Wexley yelled from the corner. "Just like Papa taught!"

Cecilia gawked when Lewis responded with a crude hand gesture, much to the amusement of the nearest spectators. How fascinating men were at times. Because of that, he took a punch to his stomach, and as she pressed her knuckles to her mouth, went so far as to bite down on one, he returned the favor, jabbing Mr. Derrickson in a shoulder and then delivering a blow that had the other man spinning about.

Then one of the things she'd most feared happened.

With a roar, Mr. Derrickson charged at the earl with fists flying. He delivered a one-two punch into Lewis' jaw and his left shoulder. Then, he either suspected that the earl was favoring that shoulder or he knew of the previous injury, for he delivered another punch to that area, and when that didn't fell the earl, he rammed his shoulder into Lewis'.

Though she heard the earl's cry of pain, she felt that pain deep in her soul. There was no way to further explain it, but her eyes filled with tears. "Oh, no." She strained against the rope to better see as Lewis fell to the ground. "Why does his arm hang at such an unnatural angle?"

Lord Wexley huffed. "It's been dislocated."

The youngest brother growled. "Why the hell did the referees not flag that? Clearly, it was an illegal charge."

The rotund judge began a countdown.

"Lewis, get up!" she yelled to the earl.

Finally, oh finally, he pushed himself to his feet. The crowd cheered.

He shook his head, but the pain on his face nearly broke her heart. As he once more circled his opponent, Cecilia clutched at Lord Frampton's arm. To be fair, he did the same to her as they both watched, frozen as Lewis delivered a few punches with his good fist.

"He's far too off balance without the use of his left arm," Lord Frampton whispered.

Lord Wexley nodded. "I agree, but he'll need to adapt, else he'll be put down."

"Come on, Lewis, just dig deep. It's almost over," she said beneath her breath as her gaze remained fixed on the earl.

Streaks of blood decorated his chest. Sweat poured down the sides of his face and neck. Pain lay etched through his expression, but he kept his feet, delivering punch after punch to Mr. Derrickson, and the last one made the greatest impression.

The bigger man staggered. One of his eyes was nearly swollen shut. Blood oozed from his nose, which Lewis had broken. Sweat made his chest and arms shiny. Clearly winded and heaving for breath, it was obvious he was nearly knackered.

And that made him reckless.

"Go down, Lethbridge," Mr. Derrickson snarled, as he circled the earl.

"You first, you bastard."

"She's mine."

"Only if I'm dead."

"That's my goal." Then the big man swung wide, stumbling as if he were drunk. Perhaps the repeated blows to his head had addled him.

Lewis easily avoided the punch, and his footwork was still impressive even though his left arm hung at an awkward and no doubt painful angle. With a cry of rage, he responded with an uppercut to the jaw that landed Mr. Derrickson onto his back.

The crowd roared.

Mr. Derrickson lay on the grass, his chest heaving as the judge and referee hurried over to his side. While some spectators yelled at him to get up, the big man lifted an arm and let it flop to the grass.

Seconds went by as everyone waited.

Cecilia could hardly breathe.

Then, the rotund little man finally rang the handbell once more. "The winner of this bout is the Earl of Lethbridge!"

Roars went through the crowd as Lewis was declared the victor.

LEWIS TRIED TO regulate his breathing as he peered down at the fallen form of Mr. Derrickson. Pain screamed through his left arm and shoulder. If he wasn't careful, he'd cast up his accounts right there in the ring, but all his concentration went into keeping his feet, and as the crowd yelled its approval for his victory, he scanned the ropes for a glimpse of Cecilia.

Oh, dear God.

She had come under the rope, quickly followed by Duncan, but she didn't stop there, and what was more, she was still clad in her ballgown covered by a cloak. When he assumed she would fly to his side, she didn't. Instead, with a cry of what he guessed was rage, she streamed past him to throw herself upon the still-down Mr. Derrickson. Without a care for her beautiful dress, she straddled the fallen man and then proceeded to beat him with her fists.

"What the hell is happening?" he asked of both Alex and Duncan as they reached his location. "Did you know she would do this?"

"Of course not," Duncan said as he frowned at Cecilia. "Perhaps she's gone insane."

"No, listen," Alex urged them both as they continued to watch her. "She's berating him."

The crowd gasped and strained. Of course gossip would fly and their names would no doubt be in the papers by evening tomorrow. However, there was nothing for it.

"Bloody hell, but she's a marvel." In significant pain and with his shoulder throbbing, he held his arm steady with his right hand, then left his brothers. "Cecilia, enough." When he reached her, he tried to pull her off the bigger man.

She, of course, ignored him in favor of landing her fists into Mr. Derrickson's cheeks and chin. "Do not think to molest me any longer because I am not for you." *Punch, smack!* "When a woman doesn't want your attention and tells you, she means it."

"Cecilia, he is not worth the continued scandal." Even now, so many men leered as her skirting crept up her legs to her knees.

She blew out a breath while the hood of her cloak fell backward, giving everyone present a view of her face. "If you ever attempt to block my path when I'm at my father's office, I will pitch you into the harbor." Then she followed the threat by driving a knee into Mr. Derrickson's groin before allowing Lewis to pull her into a standing position.

"You have made your point, sweeting," he whispered against the shell of her ear. "He won't soon forget this night." Even now, the other man groaned and remained on the ground.

Blinking, she gazed up at him as if seeing him for the first time since she'd entered the boxing ring. "Oh, Lewis!" Tears fell copiously to her cheeks, and even though he was sweaty and bloody, she flung herself into his arms—well, arm, as it were— and hugged him close. "I'm so glad you weren't killed."

"Of course I wasn't. It was merely a boxing match." Despite the intense pain, he drew her out of the ring and beneath the ropes as his brothers accompanied them. "But I won, didn't I?"

"Barely." She shook her head. "We were all concerned for you. My father came, as well as your mother."

"What?" With a glance around, he realized the captain stood nearby, looking on with amused indulgence while his brothers both nodded. "Mama is here?" He couldn't wrap his brain around the concept. "She despises boxing."

"She does," Duncan said with a chuckle. "But she stayed back with the coach. We should probably tell her that you haven't been dispatched to your death."

"Yes, of course." He gritted his teeth against the waves of pain moving through his body from all fronts. "There is something I must do first, and it can't wait." Awkwardly, and quite painfully, he dropped to his good knee while his other one screamed at him to rest. "Cecilia, darling, humor me," he said in a halting voice as he took her hand in his good one.

"Please don't do this here," she asked in a whisper. "It isn't necessary, and you need to see the doctor."

"I don't wish to waste any more time, for I realized during that fight exactly what I wanted for my future." He gazed up at her, met her cornflower blue eyes and felt the same calm he always did when in her company. "When you walked into my boxing salon nearly two weeks ago, I knew you would change my life, but I didn't know just how much."

"Oh, I…" Her words trailed off as a faint blush stained her cheeks.

"Please, sweeting, let me do this." Ignoring the pain and fighting off the darkness hovering at the edges of his vision, Lewis continued. "Over the course of our relationship, we have grown close. You have shown me a different way to see things, have quietly led me to greater heights with your determination and resolve. I admire the hell out of you, Lia, and I can't imagine going forward into the remainder of my life without you with me every step of the way."

"How lovely. You believed in me when no other man wished to help me defend myself. That immediately makes you different from them." The delicate tendons in her throat worked with a hard swallow. "What are you trying to ask of me?"

"Just this." With a glance at his brothers, who both gave nods of encouragement, he sighed. "Please marry me, Cecilia. Make me the happiest of men by wedding me and being my countess. Together, we have so much potential."

"I…" The blush in her cheeks deepened, and they'd accumulated a rather large crowd around them. "Do you think I am strong enough to withstand everything the *beau monde* might throw at me as a countess? As a woman who has no connections or a title?"

"Sweeting, there isn't a woman stronger, and I am constantly amazed by you."

"But…" She pressed her trembling lips together. "I have been led astray by men before, have been horribly treated because of that."

"You have, and I would chase down every one of them and beat them bloody for you. However, I would rather use that time to convince you how much I love you. Yes, it sounds ridiculous and fanciful for such a quick time frame, but then I'm convinced that love doesn't play by any set of rules."

A tiny giggle escaped her, and she wiped at the tears on her cheeks with her free hand. "No, it doesn't, but love doesn't lie, and it is just one thing that sets you apart from everyone else."

"If it makes a difference, there is a parure of jewelry I have in mind for you. When I don't look and feel like death, I shall give it to you."

She laughed. "Oh Lewis, I need nothing except you."

Happiness bubbled up in his tight chest. "If you accept my hand, you'll be a countess so you'll receive much more than that. And you deserve every bit of it. Let me pamper you, Lia. Let me have the right to protect you, to keep you from every bad thing in life, to love you without restriction, because I'm quite mad for you already."

"As I have said many times before. You are a good man, Lewis, so is it any wonder why I love you? Why I couldn't help but fall for you?" She shook her head. "But know this. I don't want you to fight my battles for me. I want to fight them *with* you, with us supporting each other, because we are equals."

Both of his brothers looked on with expressions of expectation.

Lewis nodded. "Does that mean you'll marry me?"

"Yes. Oh, Lewis, yes, I will marry you, and your mother will need to square with that, because I simply won't accept more disrespect. From anyone."

The crowd around them cheered.

Immediately, Duncan went into the mass, working the men and taking wagers on when the wedding would take place. He told them they could also bet at the clubs.

"God, he has no scruples, does he?" Lewis whispered, as he scrambled painfully to his feet.

Alex snorted. "Don't blame him. His skills lie in finding investors and alternative forms of funding because he is charming and charismatic." He slapped a hand to Lewis' good shoulder. "I'm glad for you. Cecilia is a force to reckon with."

"That she is." He didn't care much about scandal, for they

were already steeped neck-deep into gossip. What was one more snippet? As Alex followed Duncan through the crowd, Lewis wrapped his good arm around Cecilia. He claimed her lips to cat calls and whoops of approval. Then he rested his forehead against hers. "If you don't mind, escort me over to the doctor so he can pop my shoulder back into place, and if I pass out, have Alex bring over a bucket of water to pour over my head. I believe my strength is nearly done."

"After this, I want you in bed for at least a couple of weeks. Your body needs to rest." She stood on her toes and kissed him. "No arguments. Let me be the strong one for a few moments. I have had loads of practice."

Oddly enough, he submitted meekly to her dominance in that moment. It was rather wonderful knowing someone cared enough to take control for a time. While she slipped an arm about his waist and guided him across the grass to where the doctor waited, he couldn't help his grin. Never had he thought that opening a boxing salon would have led him to a wife and a future, but then, fate was fickle indeed.

And he couldn't be more thrilled with the results.

Epilogue

May 1, 1820
Stapleton House
Marylebone, Mayfair
London, England

L EWIS WHISTLED AS he came into the townhouse from a visit
to the boxing salon. Though he no longer boxed profession-
ally since that bout when he'd asked Cecilia to marry him, he was
still involved in the salon's operations. Truthfully, he didn't need
to be, for his brothers ran it like a well-oiled machine, but he
simply couldn't walk away from the boxing world permanently.

Not that it mattered. Never had he felt as personally fulfilled
as he was now.

Each day that went by, he counted himself fortunate to live
the life that he did. Two months shy of celebrating a third year of
marriage to the most stubborn, supportive, strong woman he'd
ever met, there was every reason to grin, for in a few months
they would expect their first child after a couple of miscarriages.

Both of his brothers had found love as well, but their stories
were more complicated and rockier than his had been. Still, the
women they'd each wed were strong and full of integrity in their
own rights, and perhaps they needed to be, for it took a certain
kind of woman to put up with a Stapleton man.

As for his mother, since she became the Dowager Countess of

Lethbridge upon his marriage, she'd had a bit of a renaissance a few months following. Not wishing to live with the newlyweds, she'd moved into a smaller townhouse in Hanover Square that she was able to acquire with the inheritance her father had left her when he'd died years before. With Lewis' assistance, she bought the property and then enjoyed herself decorating the residence and filling it with furnishings.

Now he suspected that she might be searching for a new husband, and he supported her in that endeavor, even though he worried over her making a smart match. Odd, that, in the reversal of roles.

With a nod to the butler, he handed over his greatcoat and top hat, for the day was quite rainy, then he gave the man his gloves. "Where is Lady Lethbridge this afternoon?" Usually, his wife's daily schedule was full, but she'd promised him that she would slow down now that she had been increasing for six months.

"I believe she is in the morning room. She wished to do some numbers work until Lady Wexley comes by later for tea."

"Ah, thank you." After making his way up to that room, he peered inside, and a grin split his face to see Cecilia perched on a delicate chair behind a secretary desk with a ledger book open in front of her. A couple of years earlier, she'd taken over the accounting duties from his brother Alex, and since she enjoyed wrestling with numbers, no one bid her nay. "Lia, don't you think it's time to take a rest?"

"That depends." She lifted her head, and when her gaze collided with his, she smiled. As always, when that certain suggestive light entered her eyes, awareness shivered along his skin. "Do you have plans for how I should spend my time?"

"Mmm, I can think of a few things." Once he reached her location, Lewis held out a hand. "Come sit with me for a bit."

"All right." When she slipped her fingers into his palm and he pulled her into a standing position, the familiar warmth went through his limb. "How is the salon going?"

"Well enough." After he led her to a low sofa, he saw her settled before sitting beside her. "Alexander is a shrewd manager, and since he no longer enters prize fights, all his focus is on the salon. Under his management, the client roster has grown each year."

"Your brother certainly has a head for business, which is a good thing, for his wife wouldn't stand to have a husband who wasn't at least somewhat clever." She heaved a sigh as she snuggled into his side. "By the way, the workmen finished painting the nursery suite earlier."

"Excellent news. We'll have the furniture moved in tomorrow. Did you select a nursery maid?" For the past several weeks, she had interviewed prospective candidates, for hiring help for their infant was a much sacred task.

"I did, thanks to Alex's wife." The woman had trained under a doctor, and though she couldn't formally attain a degree from a medical school, she was in the process of setting up a small practice out of their home. "There will be no need for a wet nurse; I will see to our child's feedings myself. I just couldn't bear to hand off our sweet baby to someone else and rarely see them."

It was progressive for the time, but he wholeheartedly agreed with her thinking. "Then all we need to do is wait."

"It seems an eternity." When she grinned, he felt that against the skin of his neck. "This life has been amazing is so many ways that I never anticipated," Lia said softly as she pulled back and peered into his eyes. "Who would have thought that after the horror of my previous engagement, something wonderful would eventually come my way?"

"I feel much the same." Slipping his arms about her, Lewis pulled her close. "And I fully believe everything comes off the way it is supposed to without our bumbling interference." After he pressed a kiss into her hair, he sighed. "To be honest, I had doubts as to whether I would ever marry or start a family."

"Isn't it a lovely feeling when fate manages to surprise us?"

"Yes, I suppose it is, and none of this would have been possible if you'd not come into the boxing salon three years ago." He often thought about those early days of their relationship, and knew it was a miracle unto itself that they hadn't been run out of Town for the scandal of it all. "It also shocks me that you still adore boxing now."

"I do. It is good exercise, though I don't indulge as much these days." She caressed a hand over her belly that grew more swollen with every passing week. "At least I can be near the sport thanks to the lessons we do each Wednesday."

"That was another lovely decision you guided me into." For his wife was living a dream of hers. Last year, they had finally opened a modified salon in the rear of their townhouse to provide private lessons for clients who preferred that sort of thing. Many of those who paid for the weekly lessons were the daughters of peers, simply because they'd heard Lia's own stories of how she'd come to boxing, and they wanted the same for their girls. "In fact, every positive change that has come my way has been instigated by you."

"Well, you tell me all the time what a managing baggage I am." As she chuckled, love reflected in her eyes. "Boxing and you are all I need in my life to keep me happy."

"That is good to know, for I feel much the same, though I do rather like my family even when they aggravate me." He snorted with laughter. "And I'm looking forward to meeting this babe. Whether we have a boy or a girl, our lives will change once more."

"Fate does enjoy leading us on a merry chase, hmm?" She shifted in his arms so she could better press her lips to his throat above his cravat. "I have about ninety minutes before Alex's wife comes to tea. Oh, and Duncan mentioned his wife wished to come for a visit soon; I have no idea if that is today. But would you mind spending some private time with me? We haven't been intimate for a few days."

How much did he adore his wife? "I think that is a splendid way to pass the time, but only if you're certain it won't harm the babe."

"I am quite certain. The midwife says it is safe, even soothing for the baby."

"Good." Then, with his fingertips gliding over her cheek, he dipped his head and claimed her lips with his. "It is amazing how well everything worked for the good, and I can't wait to see what happens next."

"Neither can I," Lia said as she wriggled from his hold and then stood. "But then, I'm not surprised. After all, I suspect we had love in our corner all along. It made all the difference."

Indeed, it did, and he hoped he would never take anything he'd been given for granted.

The End

About the Author

Sandra Sookoo is a *USA Today* bestselling author who firmly believes every person deserves acceptance and a happy ending. Most days you can find her creating scandal and mischief in the Regency-era, serendipity and happenstance in Victorian America or snarky, sweet humor in the contemporary world. Most recently she's moved into infusing her books with mystery and intrigue. Reading is a lot like eating fine chocolates—you can't just have one. Good thing books don't have calories!

When she's not wearing out computer keyboards, Sandra spends time with her real-life Prince Charming in central Indiana where she's been known to goof off and make moments count because the key to life is laughter. A Disney fan since the age of ten, when her soul gets bogged down and her imagination flags, a trip to Walt Disney World is in order. Nothing fuels her dreams more than the land of eternal happy endings, hope and love stories.

Stay in Touch

Sign up for Sandra's bi-monthly newsletter and you'll be given exclusive excerpts, cover reveals before the general public as well as opportunities to enter contests you won't find anywhere else.

Just send an email to sandrasookoo@yahoo.com with SUB-SCRIBE in the subject line.

Or follow / friend her on social media:
Facebook: facebook.com / sandra.sookoo
Facebook Author Page: facebook.com / sandrasookooauthor
Pinterest: pinterest.com / sandrasookoo
Instagram: instagram.com / sandrasookoo
BookBub Page: bookbub.com / authors / sandra-sookoo

www.ingramcontent.com/pod-product-compliance
Lightning Source LLC
Chambersburg PA
CBHW060449310726

48977CB00001B/369